Readers are howling the praises of Darren Shan's DEMONATA series:

"Readers who devour Shan's Cirque Du Freak books will be snapping like werewolves themselves to get this book."

—*VOYA*

"Guaranteed to gross out anyone."

—*School Library Journal*

"The pace is non-stop, keeping the reader turning pages at a breathtaking rate."

—*Kirkus*

"Older fans of Shan's gory, gripping Cirque Du Freak series will welcome . . . the Demonata series, which features the same horrific spin, dark humor, and graphic detail."

—*Booklist*

"Gross as well as engrossing. . . . Horror fans will eat it up."

—*KLIATT*

Also in

THE DEMONATA

series:

✠   ✠   ✠

For:
Bas — my demon lover

OBEs (Order of the Bloody Entrails) to:
Caroline "pie chart" Paul
D.O.M.I.N.I.C. Kingston
Nicola "schumacher" Blacoe

Editorial Evilness:
Stellasaurus Paskins

Agents of Chaos:
the Christopher Little crew

THE DEMONATA

LORD LOSS

BY DARREN SHAN

Ⓛ Ⓑ

Little, Brown and Company
New York   Boston

Little, Brown and Company

Hachette Book Group
237 Park Avenue, New York, NY 10017
Visit our website at www.lb-teens.com

Little, Brown and Company is a division of Hachette Book Group, Inc.
The Little, Brown name and logo are trademarks of Hachette Book Group, Inc.

First U.S. Paperback Edition: May 2006

First published in Great Britain by Collins in 2005

The characters and events portrayed in this book are fictitious.
Any similarity to real persons, living or dead, is coincidental
and not intended by the author.

Library of Congress Cataloging-in-Publication Data
Shan, Darren.
Lord Loss / Darren Shan. — 1st U.S. ed.
p. cm. — (The demonata; bk. 1)
Summary: Presumably the only witness to the horrific and bloody
murder of his entire family, a teenage boy must outwit not only the
mental health professionals determined to cure his delusion, but also
the demonic forces only he can see.
ISBN 978-0-316-11499-8 (hc) / ISBN 978-0-316-01233-1 (pb)
[1. Demonology — Fiction. 2. Horror stories.] I. Title.
PZ7.S52823Lor 2005
[Fic] — dc22   2005000145

HC: 10 9 8 7 6 5 4 3 2 1
PB: 10 9 8 7 6

RRD-H

Printed in the United States of America

LORD LOSS

Lord Loss sows all the sorrows of the world
Lord Loss seeds the grief-starched trees

In the center of the web, lowly Lord Loss bows his head

Mangled hands, naked eyes
Fanged snakes his soul line
Curled inside like textured sin
Bloody, curdled sheets for skin

In the center of the web, vile Lord Loss torments the dead

Over strands of red, Lord Loss crawls
Dispensing pain, despising all
Shuns friends, nurtures foes
Ravages hope, breeds woe
Drinks moons, devours suns
Twirls his thumbs till the reaper comes

In the center of the web, lush Lord Loss is all that's left

RAT GUTS

✠   ✠   ✠

DOUBLE history on a Wednesday afternoon — total nightmare! A few minutes ago, I would have said I couldn't imagine anything worse. But when there's a knock at the door, and it opens, and I spot my Mom outside, I realize — life can always get worse.

When a parent turns up at school, unexpected, it means one of two things. Either somebody close to you has been seriously injured or has died, or you're in trouble.

My immediate reaction: Please don't let anybody be dead! I think of Dad, Gret, uncles, aunts, cousins. It could be any of them. Alive and kicking this morning. Now stiff and cold, tongue sticking out, a slab of dead meat just waiting to be buried. I remember Grandma's funeral. The open coffin. Her shining flesh, having to kiss her forehead, the pain, the tears. Please don't let anyone be dead! Please. Please. Please. Ple —

Then I see Mom's face, white with rage, and I know she's here to punish, not comfort.

I groan, roll my eyes, and mutter under my breath, "Bring on the corpses!"

✠ The principal's office. Me, Mom, and Mr. Donnellan. Mom's ranting and raving about cigarettes. I've been seen smoking behind the bike shed (the oldest cliché in the book). She wants to know if the head's aware of this, of what the pupils in his school are getting up to.

I feel a bit sorry for Mr. Donnellan. He has to sit there, looking like a schoolboy himself, shuffling his feet and saying he didn't know this was going on and he'll launch an investigation and put a quick end to it. Liar! Of course he knew. Every school has a smoking area. That's life. Teachers don't approve, but they turn a blind eye most of the time. Certain kids smoke — fact. Safer to have them smoking at school than sneaking off the grounds during breaks and at lunch.

Mom knows that too. She must! She was young once, like she's always reminding me. Kids were no different in Mom's time. If she stopped for a minute and thought back, she'd see what an embarrassment she's being. I wouldn't mind her harassing me at home, but you don't march into school and start laying down the law in the principal's office. She's out of order — big time.

But it's not like I can tell her, is it? I can't pipe up with, "Hey! Mother! You're disgracing us both, so shut yer trap!"

I smirk at the thought, and of course that's when Mom pauses for the briefest of moments and catches me. "What are you grinning at?" she roars, and then she's off again — I'm smoking myself into an early grave, the school's responsible, what sort of a freak show is Mr. Donnellan running, la-di-la-di-la-di-bloody-la!

BAW*ring*.

✠ Her rant at school's nothing compared to the one I get at home. Screaming at the top of her lungs, blue bloody murder. She's going to send me off to boarding school — no, military school! See how I like that, having to get up at dawn each morning and do a hundred push-ups before breakfast. How does *that* sound?

"Is breakfast bacon and eggs or some cereally, yogurty crap?" is my response, and I know the second it's out of my mouth that it's the wrong thing to say. This isn't the time for the famed Grubbs Grady brand of cutting-edge humor.

Cue the enraged Mom fireworks. Who do I think I am? Do I *know* how much they spend on me? What if I get kicked out of school? Then the clincher, the one Moms all over the world love pulling out of the hat — "Just wait till your father gets home!"

✠ Dad's not as freaked out as Mom, but he's not happy. He tells me how disappointed he is. They've warned me so many times about the dangers of smoking, how it destroys people's lungs and gives them cancer.

"Smoking's dumb," he says. We're in the kitchen (I haven't been out of it since Mom dragged me home from school early, except to go to the toilet). "It's disgusting, antisocial, and lethal. Why do it, Grubbs? I thought you had more sense."

I shrug wordlessly. What's there to say? They're being

unfair. *Of course* smoking's dumb. *Of course* it gives you cancer. *Of course* I shouldn't be doing it. But my friends smoke. It's cool. You get to hang out with cool people at lunch and talk about cool things. But only if you smoke. You can't be *in* if you're *out*. And they know that. Yet here they stand, acting all Gestapo, asking me to account for my actions.

"How long has he been smoking? That's what I want to know!" Mom's started referring to me in the third person since Dad arrived. I'm beneath direct mention.

"Yes," Dad says. "How long, Grubbs?"

"I dunno."

"Weeks? Months? Longer?"

"A few months maybe. But only a couple a day."

"If he says a couple, he means at least five or six," Mom snorts.

"No, I don't!" I shout. "I mean a couple!"

"Don't raise your voice to me!" Mom roars back.

"Easy," Dad begins, but Mom goes on as if he isn't there.

"Do you think it's clever? Filling your lungs with rubbish, killing yourself? We didn't bring you up to watch you give yourself cancer! We don't need this, certainly not at this time, not when —"

"Enough!" Dad shouts, and we both jump. Dad almost never shouts. He usually gets very quiet when he's angry. Now his face is red and he's glaring — but at both of us, not just me.

Mom coughs, as if she's ashamed of herself. She sits, brushes her hair back off her face, and looks at me with wounded eyes. I hate when she pulls a face like this. It's impossible to look at her straight or argue.

"I want you to stop, Grubbs," Dad says, back in control now. "We're not going to punish you —" Mom starts to object, but Dad silences her with a curt wave of his hand "— but I want your word that you'll stop. I know it won't be easy. I know your friends will give you a hard time. But this is important. Some things matter more than looking cool. Will you promise, Grubbs?" He pauses. "Of course, that's if you're *able* to quit . . ."

"Of course I'm able," I mutter. "I'm not addicted or anything."

"Then will you? For *your* sake — not ours?"

I shrug, trying to act like it's no big thing, like I was planning to stop anyway. "Sure, if you're going to make that much of a fuss about it." I yawn.

Dad smiles. Mom smiles. I smile.

Then Gret walks in the back door and she's smiling too — but it's an evil, big-sister-superior smile. "Have we sorted all our little problems out yet?" she asks, voice high and fake-innocent.

And I know instantly — Gret told on me to Mom. She found out that I was smoking and she told. The pig!

As she swishes past, beaming like an angel, I burn fiery holes in the back of her head with my eyes, and a single word echoes through my head like the sound of ungodly thunder . . .

Revenge!

✠ I love garbage dumps. You can find all sorts of disgusting stuff there. The perfect place to go browsing if you want to get even with your annoying traitor of a sister. I climb over mounds of garbage and root through black bags and soggy cardboard boxes. I'm not sure exactly what I'm going to use, or in what fashion, so I wait for inspiration to strike. Then, in a small plastic bag, I find six dead rats, necks broken, just starting to rot. *Excellent.*

Look out, Gret — here I come!

✠ Eating breakfast at the kitchen table. Radio turned down low. Listening to the noises upstairs. Trying not to chuckle. Waiting for the outburst.

Gret's in her shower. She showers at least twice a day, before she goes to school and when she gets back. Sometimes she has one before going to bed too. I don't know why anybody would bother to keep themselves so clean. I figure it's a form of madness.

Because she's so obsessed with showering, Mom and Dad gave her the *en suite* bedroom. They figured I wouldn't mind. And I don't. In fact, it's perfect. I wouldn't have been able to pull my trick if Gret didn't have her own shower, with its very own towel rack.

The shower goes off. Splatters, then drips, then silence. I tense with excitement. I know Gret's routines inside out. She always pulls her towel down off its rack *after* she's showered, not before. I can't hear her footsteps, but I imagine her taking the three or four steps to the towel rack. Reaching up. Pulling it down. Aaaaaaaaannnddd . . .

On cue — screams galore. A shocked single scream to start. Then a volley of them, one running into another. I push my bowl of soggy cornflakes aside and prepare myself for the biggest laugh of the year.

Mom and Dad are by the sink, discussing the day ahead. They go stiff when they hear the screams, then dash towards the stairs, which I can see from where I'm sitting.

Gret appears before they reach the stairs. Crashes out of her room, screaming, slapping bloody shreds from her arms, tearing them from her hair. She's covered in red. Towel clutched with one hand over her front — even terrified out of her wits, there's no way she's going to come down naked!

"What's wrong?" Mom shouts. "What's happening?"

"Blood!" Gret screams. "I'm covered in blood! I pulled the towel down. I . . ."

She stops. She's spotted me laughing. I'm doubled over. It's the funniest thing I've ever seen.

Mom turns and looks at me. Dad does too. They're speechless.

Gret picks a sticky pink chunk out of her hair, slowly this time, and studies it. "What did you put on my towel?" she asks quietly.

"Rat guts!" I howl, pounding the table, crying with laughter. "I got . . . rats at the dump . . . chopped them up . . . and . . ." I almost get sick, I'm laughing so much.

Mom stares at me. Dad stares at me. Gret stares at me. Then —

"You lousy son of a — !"

I don't catch the rest of the insult — Gret flies down the stairs ahead of it. She drops her towel on the way. I don't have time to react to that before she's on me, slapping and scratching at my face.

"What's wrong, *Gretelda*?" I giggle, fending her off, calling her by the name she hates. She normally calls me Grubitsch in response, but she's too mad to think of it now.

"Scum!" she shrieks. Then she lunges at me sharply, grabs my jaw, jerks my mouth open, and tries her hardest to stuff a handful of rat guts down my throat.

I stop laughing instantly — a mouthful of rotten rat guts wasn't part of the grand über-joke. "Get off!" I roar, lashing out wildly. Mom and Dad suddenly recover and shout at exactly the same time.

"Stop that!"

"Don't hit your sister!"

"She's a lunatic," I gasp, pushing myself away from the steaming Gret, falling off my chair.

"He's an animal," Gret sobs, picking more chunks of guts from her hair, wiping rat blood from her face. I realize she's crying — serious waterworks — and her face is as red as her long, straight hair. Not red from the blood — red from anger, shame and . . . *fear*?

Mom picks up the dropped towel, takes it to Gret, wraps it around her. Dad's just behind them, face as dark as death. Gret picks more strands and loops of rat guts from her hair, then howls with anguish.

"They're all over me!" she yells, then throws some of the guts at me. "You stinky little monster!"

"*You're* the one who's *stinky!*" I cackle. Gret dives for my throat.

"No more!" Dad doesn't raise his voice but his tone stops us dead.

Mom's staring at me with open disgust. Dad's shooting

daggers. I sense that I'm the only one who sees the funny side of this.

"It was just a joke," I mutter defensively before the accusations fly.

"I hate you," Gret hisses, then bursts into fresh tears and flees dramatically.

"Cal," Mom says to Dad, freezing me with an ice-cold glare. "Take Grubitsch in hand. I'm going up to try and comfort Gretelda." Mom always calls us by our given names. She's the one who picked them, and is the only person in the world who doesn't see how shudderingly awful they are.

Mom heads upstairs. Dad sighs, walks to the counter, tears off several sheets of kitchen paper, and mops up some of the guts and streaks of blood from the floor. After a couple of silent minutes of this, as I lie uncertainly by my upturned chair, he turns his steely gaze on me. Lots of sharp lines around his mouth and eyes — the sign that he's *really* angry, even angrier than he was about me smoking.

"You shouldn't have done that," he says.

"It was funny," I mutter.

"No," he barks. "It wasn't."

"She deserved it!" I cry. "She's done worse to me! She told Mom about me smoking — I know it was her. And remember the time she melted my lead soldiers? And cut up my comics? And —"

"There are some things you should never do," Dad interrupts softly. "This was *wrong*. You invaded your sister's privacy, humiliated her, terrified her senseless. And the timing! You . . ." He pauses and ends with a fairly weak ". . . upset her greatly." He checks his watch. "Get ready for school. We'll discuss your punishment later."

I trudge upstairs miserably, unable to see what all the aggro is about. It was a great joke. I laughed for hours when I thought of it. And all that hard work — chopping the rats up, mixing in some water to keep them fresh and make them gooey, getting up early, sneaking into her bathroom while she was asleep, carefully putting the guts in place — wasted.

I pass Gret's bedroom and hear her crying pitifully. Mom's whispering softly to her. My stomach gets hard, the way it does when I know I've done something bad. I ignore it. "I don't care what they say," I grumble, kicking open the door to my room and tearing off my pajamas. "It was a brilliant joke."

✠ Purgatory. Confined to my room after school for a month. A whole bloody *MONTH*! No TV, no computer, no comics, no books — except schoolbooks. Dad leaves my chess set in the room too — no fear my chess-crazy parents would take *that* away from me! Chess is almost a religion in this house. Gret and I were reared on it. While other toddlers were being taught how to put jigsaws together, we were busy learning the ridiculous rules of chess.

I can come downstairs for meals, and bathroom visits are allowed, but otherwise I'm a prisoner. I can't even go out on the weekends.

In solitude, I call Gret every name under the moon the first night. Mom and Dad bear the brunt of my curses the next. After that I'm too miserable to blame anyone, so I sulk in moody silence and play chess against myself to pass the time.

They don't talk to me at meals. The three of them act like I'm not there. Gret doesn't even glance at me spitefully and sneer, the way she usually does when I'm getting the dog-house treatment.

But what have I done that's so bad? OK, it was a crude joke and I knew I'd get into trouble — but their reactions are waaaaaaay over the top. If I'd done something to embarrass Gret in public, fair enough, I'd take what was coming. But this was a private joke, just between us. They shouldn't be making such a song and dance about it.

Dad's words echo back to me — "And the timing!" I think about them a lot. And Mom's, when she was going on about smoking, just before Dad cut her short — "We don't need this, certainly not at this time, not when —"

What did they mean? What were they talking about? What does the timing have to do with anything?

Something stinks here — and it's not just rat guts.

✠ I spend a lot of time writing. Diary entries, stories, poems. I try drawing a comic — "Grubbs Grady, Superhero!" — but I'm no good at art. I get great marks in my other subjects — way better than goat-faced Gret ever gets, as I often remind her — but I've got all the artistic talent of a duck.

I play lots of games of chess. Mom and Dad are chess fanatics. There's a board in every room and they play several games most nights, against each other or friends from their chess clubs. They make Gret and me play too. My earliest memory is of sucking on a white rook while Dad explained how a knight moves.

I can beat just about anyone my age — I've won regional competitions — but I'm not in the same class as Mom, Dad, or Gret. Gret's won at national level and can wipe the floor with me nine times out of ten. I've only ever beaten Mom twice in my life. Dad — never.

It's been the biggest argument starter all my life. Mom and Dad don't put pressure on me to do well in school or at other games, but they press me all the time at chess. They make me read chess books and watch videotaped tournaments. We have long debates over meals and in Dad's study about legendary games and grandmasters, and how I can improve. They send me to tutors and keep entering me in competitions. I've argued with them about it — I'd rather spend my time watching and playing soccer — but they've always stood firm.

White rook takes black pawn, threatens black queen. Black queen moves to safety. I chase her with my bishop. Black queen moves again — still in danger. This is childish stuff — I could have cut off the threat five moves back, when it became apparent — but I don't care. In a petty way, this is me striking back. "You take my TV and computer away? Stick me up here on my own? OK — I'm gonna learn to play the worst game of chess in the world. See how you like that, Corporal Dad and Commandant Mom!"

Not exactly Luke Skywalker striking back against the evil Empire by blowing up the *Death Star*, I know, but hey, we've all gotta start somewhere!

✚ Studying my hair in the mirror. Stiff, tight, ginger. Dad used to be ginger when he was younger, before the grey set in. Says he was fifteen or sixteen when he noticed the change. So, if I follow in his footsteps, I've only got a handful or so years of unbroken ginger to look forward to.

I like the idea of a few grey hairs, not a whole head of them like Dad, just a few. And spread out — I don't want a skunk patch. I'm big for my age — taller than most of my friends — and burly. I don't look old, but if I had a few grey hairs, I might be able to pass for an adult in poor light — bluff my way into R-rated movies!

The door opens. Gret — smiling shyly. I'm nineteen days into my sentence. Full of hate for Gretelda Grotesque. She's the last person I want to see.

"Get out!"

"I came to make up," she says.

"Too late," I snarl nastily. "I've only got eleven days to go. I'd rather see them out than kiss your . . ." I stop. She's holding out a plastic bag. Something blue inside. "What's that?" I ask suspiciously.

"A present to make up for getting you grounded," she says, and lays it on my bed. She glances out of the window. The curtains are open. A three-quarters moon lights up the sill. There are some chess pieces on it, from when I was playing earlier. Gret shivers, then turns away.

"Mom and Dad said you can come out — the punishment's over. They've ended it early."

She leaves.

Bewildered, I tear open the plastic. Inside — a Brazil jersey, shorts, and socks. I'm stunned. Brazil is my favorite soccer team. Mom used to buy me their latest gear at the start of every season, until I hit puberty and sprouted. She won't buy me any new gear until I stop growing — I outgrew the last one in just a month.

This must have cost Gret a fortune — it's brand new, not last season's. This is the first time she's ever given me a present, except at Christmas and birthdays. And Mom and Dad have never cut short a grounding before — they're very strict about making us stick to any punishment they set.

What the hell is going on?

✠ Three days after my early release. To say things are strange is the understatement of the decade. The atmosphere's just like it was when Grandma died. Mom and Dad wander around like robots, not saying much. Gret mopes in her room or in the kitchen, stuffing herself with sweets and playing chess nonstop. She's like an addict. It's bizarre.

I want to ask them about it, but how? "Mom, Dad — have aliens taken over your bodies? Is somebody dead and you're too afraid to tell me? Have you all converted to Misery-ism?"

Seriously, jokes aside, I'm frightened. They're sharing a secret, something bad, and keeping me out of it. Why? Is it to do with me? Do they know something that I don't? Like maybe . . . maybe . . .

(Go on — have the guts! Say it!)

Like maybe *I'm* going to die?

Stupid? An overreaction? Reading too much into it? Per-haps. But they cut short my punishment. Gret gave me a present. They look like they're about to burst into tears at any given minute.

Grubbs Grady — on his way out? A deadly disease I caught on vacation? A brain defect I've had since birth? The big, bad Cancer bug?

What other explanation is there?

✠ "Regale me with your thoughts on ballet."

I'm watching soccer highlights. Alone in the TV room with Dad. I cock my ear at the weird, out-of-nowhere question and shrug. "Rubbish," I snort.

"You don't think it's an incredibly beautiful art form? You've never wished to experience it firsthand? You don't want to glide across Swan Lake or get sweet with a Nut-cracker?"

I choke on a laugh. "Is this a windup?"

Dad smiles. "Just wanted to check. I got a great offer on tickets to a performance tomorrow. I bought three — antic-ipating your less-than-enthusiastic reaction — but I could probably get an extra one if you want to tag along."

"No way!"

"Your loss." Dad clears his throat. "The ballet's out of town and finishes quite late. It will be easier for us to stay in a hotel overnight."

"Does that mean I'll have the house to myself?" I ask ex-citedly.

"No such luck," he chuckles. "I think you're old enough to guard the fort, but Sharon" — Mom — "has a different view, and she's the boss. You'll have to stay with Aunt Kate."

"Not no-date Kate," I groan. Aunt Kate's only a couple of years older than Mom, but lives like a ninety-year-old. Has a black-and-white TV but only turns it on for the news. Listens to radio the rest of the time. "Couldn't I kill myself instead?" I quip.

"Don't make jokes like that!" Dad snaps with unexpected venom. I stare at him, hurt, and he forces a thin smile. "Sorry. Hard day at the office. I'll arrange it with Kate, then."

He stumbles as he exits — as if he's nervous. For a minute there it was like normal, me and Dad messing around, and I forgot all my recent worries. Now they come flooding back. If I'm not at death's door, why was he so upset at my throw-away gag?

Curious and afraid, I slink to the door and eavesdrop as he phones Aunt Kate and clears my stay with her. Nothing suspicious in their conversation. He doesn't talk about me as if these are my final days. Even hangs up with a cheery "Toodle-oo," a corny phrase he often uses on the phone. I'm about to withdraw and catch up with the soccer action when I hear Gret speaking softly from the stairs.

"He didn't want to come?"

"No," Dad whispers back.

"It's all set?"

"Yes. He'll stay with Kate. It'll just be the three of us."

"Couldn't we wait until next month?"

"Best to do it now — it's too dangerous to put off."

"I'm scared, Dad."

"I know, love. So am I."

Silence.

✣ Mom drops me off at Aunt Kate's. They exchange some small talk on the doorstep, but Mom's in a rush and cuts the chat short. Says she has to hurry or they'll be late for the ballet. Aunt Kate buys that, but I've cracked their cover story. I don't know what Mom and Co. are up to tonight, but they're not going to watch a load of poseurs in tights jumping around like puppets.

"Be good for your aunt," Mom says, tweaking the hairs on my fringe.

"Enjoy the ballet," I reply, smiling hollowly.

Mom hugs me, then kisses me. I can't remember the last time she kissed me. There's something desperate about it.

"I love you, Grubitsch!" she croaks, almost sobbing.

If I hadn't already known something was very, very wrong, the dread in her voice would have tipped me off. Prepared for it, I'm able to grin and flip back at her, Humphrey Bogart style, "Love you too, shweetheart."

Mom drives away. I think she's crying.

"Make yourself comfy in the living room," Aunt Kate simpers. "I'll fix a nice pot of tea for us. It's almost time for the news."

✠ I make an excuse after the news. Sore stomach — need to rest. Aunt Kate makes me gulp down two large spoons of cod liver oil, then sends me up to bed.

I wait five minutes, until I hear Frank Sinatra crooning — no-date Kate loves Ol' Blue Eyes and always manages to find him on the radio. When I hear her singing along to some corny ballad, I slip downstairs and out the front door.

I don't know what's going on, but now that I know I'm not set to go toes-up, I'm determined to see it through with them. I don't care what sort of a mess they're in. I won't let

Mom, Dad, and Gret freeze me out, no matter how bad it is. We're a family. We should face things together. That's what Mom and Dad always taught me.

Padding through the streets, covering the four miles home as quickly as I can. They could be anywhere, but I'll start with the house. If I don't find them there, I'll look for clues to where they might be.

I think of Dad saying he's scared. Mom trembling as she kissed me. Gret's voice when she was on the stairs. My stomach tightens with fear. I ignore it, jog at a steady pace, and try spitting the taste of cod liver oil out of my mouth.

✠ Home. I spot a chink of light in Mom and Dad's bedroom, where the curtains just fail to meet. It doesn't mean they're in — Mom always leaves a light on to deter burglars. I slip around the back and peer through the garage window. The car's parked inside. So they're here. This is where it all kicks off. Whatever "it" is.

I creep up to the back door. Crouch, poke the dog flap open, listen for sounds. None. I was eight when our last dog died. Mom said she was never allowing another one inside the house — they always got killed on the roads and she was sick of burying them. Every few months, Dad says he must board over the dog flap or get a new door, but he never has. I think he's still secretly hoping she'll change her mind. Dad loves dogs.

When I was a baby, I could crawl through the flap. Mom had to keep me tied to the kitchen table to stop me sneaking out of the house when she wasn't looking. Much too big for it now, so I fish under the pyramid-shaped stone to the left of the door and locate the spare key.

The kitchen's cold. It shouldn't be — the sun's been shining all day and it's a nice warm night — but it's like standing in a refrigerator aisle in a supermarket.

I creep to the hall door and stop, again listening for sounds. None.

Leaving the kitchen, I check the TV room, Mom's fancily decorated living room — off-limits to Gret and me except on special occasions — and Dad's study. Empty. All as cold as the kitchen.

Coming out of the study, I notice something strange and do a double-take. There's a chess board in one corner. Dad's prize chess set. The pieces are based on characters from the King Arthur legends. Hand-carved by some famous craftsman in the nineteenth century. Cost a fortune. Dad never told Mom the exact price — never dared.

I walk to the board. Carved out of marble, four inches thick. I played a game with Dad on its smooth surface just a few weeks ago. Now it's scarred by deep, ugly gouges. Almost like fingernail scratches — except no human could drag their nails through solid marble. And all the carefully crafted pieces are missing. The board's bare.

Up the stairs. Sweating nervously. Fingers clenched tight. My breath comes out as mist before my eyes. Part of me wants to turn tail and run. I shouldn't be here. I don't *need* to be here. Nobody would know if I backed up and . . .

I flash back to Gret's face after the rat guts prank. Her tears. Her pain. Her smile when she gave me the Brazil jersey. We fight all the time, but I love her deep down. And not that deep either.

I'm not going to leave her alone with Mom and Dad to face whatever trouble they're in. Like I told myself earlier — we're a family. Dad's always said families should pull together and fight as a team. I want to be part of this — even though I don't know what "this" is, even though Mom and Dad did all they could to keep me out of "this," even though "this" terrifies me senseless.

The landing. Not as cold as downstairs. I try my bedroom, then Gret's. Empty. Very warm. The chess pieces on Gret's board are also missing. Mine haven't been taken, but they lie scattered on the floor and my board has been smashed to splinters.

I edge closer to Mom and Dad's room. I've known all along that this is where they must be. Delaying the moment of truth. Gret likes to call me a coward when she wants to hurt me. Big as I am, I've always gone out of my way to avoid fights. I used to think (*fear*) she might be right. Each step I take towards my parents' bedroom proves to my surprise that she was wrong.

The door feels red hot, as though a fire is burning behind it. I press an ear to the wood — if I hear the crackle of flames, I'll race straight to the phone and dial the emergency number. But there's no crackle. No smoke. Just deep, heavy breathing . . . and a curious dripping sound.

My hand's on the doorknob. My fingers won't move. I keep my ear pressed to the wood, waiting . . . praying. A tear trickles from my left eye. It dries on my cheek from the heat.

Inside the room, somebody giggles — low, throaty, sadistic. Not Mom, Dad, or Gret. There's a ripping sound, followed by snaps and crunches.

My hand turns.

The door opens.

Hell is revealed.

DEMONS

✠   ✠   ✠

Blood everywhere. Nightmarish splashes and gory pools. Wild streaks across the floor and walls.

Except the walls aren't walls. I'm surrounded on all four sides by *webs*. Millions of strands, thicker than my arm, some connecting in orderly designs, others running chaotically apart. Many of the strands are stained with blood. Behind the layer of webs, more layers — banks of them stretching back as far as I can see. Infinite.

My eyes snap from the walls. I make quick, mental thumbnails of other details. Numb. Functioning like a machine.

The dripping sound — a body hanging upside down from the webby ceiling in the center of the room. No head. Blood drops to the floor from the gaping red O of the neck. Even without the head, I recognize him.

"*DAD!*" I scream, and the cry almost rips my vocal chords apart.

To my left, an obscene creature spins round and snarls. It

has the body of a very large dog, the head of a crocodile. Beneath it, motionless — Mom. Or what's left of her.

A dreadful howl to my right. Gret! Sitting on the floor, staring at me, weaving sideways, her face white, except where it's smeared with blood. I start to call to her. She half-turns, and I realize that she's been split in two. Something's behind her, in the cavity at the back, moving her like a hand puppet.

The "something" pushes Gret away. It's a child, but no child of this world. It has the body of a three-year-old, with a head much larger than any normal person's. Pale green skin. No eyes — a small ball of fire flickers in each of its empty sockets. No hair — yet its head is alive with movement. As the hell-child advances, I see that the objects on its head are cockroaches. Living. Feeding on its rotten flesh.

The crocodile-dog moves away from Mom and also closes in on me, exchanging glances with the monstrous child, who's narrowing the gap.

I can't move. Fear has seized me completely. I look from Mom to Dad to Gret. All red. All dead.

Impossible! This isn't happening! A bad dream — it *must* be!

But even in my very worst nightmare, I never imagined anything like this. I know that it's real, simply because it's too awful not to be.

The creatures are almost upon me. The croc-dog growls hungrily. The child grins ghoulishly and raises its hands — there are mouths in both its palms, small, full of sharp teeth. No tongues.

"Oh dear," someone says, and the creatures stop within spitting distance. "What have we here?"

A man slides out from behind a clump of webby strands. Thin. Pale red skin, misshapen, lumpy, as though made out of colored dough. His hands are mangled, bones sticking out of the skin, one finger melting into another. Bald. Strange eyes — no white, just a dark red iris and an even darker pupil. There's a gaping, jagged hole in the left side of his chest. I can look clean through it. Inside the hole — snakes. Dozens of tiny, hissing, coiled serpents, with long curved fangs.

The hell-child shrieks and reaches towards me. The teeth in its small mouths are eagerly snapping open and shut.

"Stop, Artery," the man — the *monster* — says commandingly, and steps towards me. No . . . he doesn't step . . . he *glides.* He has no feet. The lumpy flesh of his lower legs ends in sharp strips that don't touch the floor. He's hovering in the air.

The croc-dog barks savagely, its reptilian eyes alive with hunger and hate.

"Hold, Vein," the monster orders. He advances to within touching distance of me. Stops and studies me with his unnatural red eyes. He has a small mouth. White lips. He looks sad — the saddest creature I've ever seen.

"You are Grubitsch," he says morosely. "The last of the Gradys. You should not be here. Your parents wished to spare you this heartache. Why did you come?"

I can't answer. My body isn't my own, except my eyes, which don't stop roaming and analyzing, even though I want them to — easier to shut off completely and black everything out.

The hell-child makes a guttural sound and reaches for me again.

"Disobey me at your peril, Artery," the monster says

softly. The barbaric baby drops its hands and shuffles backwards, the fire in its eyes dimming. The croc-dog retreats too. Both keep their sights on me.

"Such sadness," the monster sighs, and there's genuine pity in his tone. "Parents — dead. Sister — dead. All alone in the world. Face to face with demons. No idea who we are or why we're here." He pauses, and doubt crosses his expression. "You *don't* know, do you, Grubitsch? Nobody ever explained, or told you the story of lonely Lord Loss?"

I still can't answer, but he reads the ignorance in my eyes and smiles thinly, painfully. "I thought not," he says. "They sought to protect you from the cruelties of the world. Good, loving parents. You'll miss them, Grubitsch — but not for long." The creatures to my left and right make sick, chuckling sounds. "Your sorrow shall be short-lived. Within minutes I'll set my familiars upon you and all will soon finish. There will be pain — great pain — but then the total peace of the beyond. Death will come as a blessing, Grubitsch. You will welcome it in the end — as your parents and sister did."

The monster drifts around me. I realize he has no nose, just two large holes above his upper lip. He sniffs as he passes, and I somehow understand that he's smelling my fear.

"Poor Grubitsch," he murmurs, stopping in front of me again. This close, I can see that his red skin is broken by tiny cracks, seeping with drops of blood. I also notice several appendages beneath his arms — three on either side, folded around his stomach. They look like thin, extra arms, though they might just be oddly molded layers of flesh.

"Wh-wh . . . what . . . are . . . you?" I moan, forcing the words out between my chattering teeth.

"The beginning and end of your greatest sorrows," the monster replies. He says it plainly — not a boast.

"Mu-Mom?" I gasp. "Dad? Gr-Gr . . . Gr . . ."

"Gone," he whispers, shaking his head, blood oozing from the cracks in his neck. "Remember them, Grubitsch. Recall the golden memories. Cherish them in these, your final moments. Cry for them, Grubitsch. Give me your tears."

He smiles eagerly and his right hand reaches for my face. He brushes his mashed-together fingers across my left cheek, just beneath my eye, as though trying to charm tears from me.

The touch of his skin — moist, rough, sticky — repels me. Without thinking, I turn my back on the hell of my parents' bedroom and run. Behind me, the monster chuckles darkly, clears his throat, and says, "Vein. Artery. He is yours."

With vile, vicious howls of delight, the creatures give chase.

✠ The landing. Growls and grinding teeth getting closer every second. Almost upon me. My legs slip. I sprawl to the floor. Something flies overhead and collides with the wall at the top of the stairs — the croc-dog, Vein.

A tiny hand snags on my left ankle. Artery's teeth close on the cuffs of my jeans. I pull away instinctively. Ripping — a long strip of material torn clean away. No damage to my leg. Artery rolls backwards, choking on the denim.

Vein scrambles to its feet, shaking its elongated crocodile's head. My eyes fix on its legs. They don't end in dog's paws, but in tiny human hands, with long, blood-stained, splintered nails — a woman's.

I wriggle past Vein on my stomach and drag myself down

the stairs, gasping with terror. Out of the corner of my eye I spy Artery spitting out the denim, jumping to his feet, rushing after me.

Vein crouches at the top of the stairs, reptilian eyes furious, readying itself — *herself* — to pounce. Just as she leaps, Artery crashes into her. Vein yelps as her companion accidentally crushes her against the wall. Artery wails like a baby, kicks Vein out of the way, and totters down the stairs in pursuit of me.

My hands hit floor. I lurch to my feet and start for the front door. I've a good lead on Artery, who's still on the stairs. I'm going to make it! A few more strides and . . .

Something brushes between my legs at an incredible speed. There's a sharp clattering sound. The door shakes. At its base, Artery rights himself and grins at me. The grotesque hell-child is rubbing his right shoulder, where he collided with the door. The fire in his eyes burns brighter than ever. His mouth is wide and twisted. No tongue — just a gaping, blood-red maw.

I scream incoherently at Artery, then grab the telephone from its stand — the closest object to hand — and lob it with all my strength at the demon. Artery ducks sharply. Unbelievably, the telephone smashes through the door, ending up in the street outside.

I have no time to ponder this impossible feat of strength. Artery's momentarily disoriented. Vein's only halfway down the stairs. I can escape — *if* I act quickly.

Making a sharp turn, I dive for the kitchen and the back door. Artery reads my intentions and bellows at Vein. The croc-dog leaps from the stairs and sails for my face and throat. I bring up an arm and swat her away. Vein's nails catch on my arm, rip through the material of my shirt and make three deep gouges in the flesh of my forearm.

Yelling with pain, I kick out at the demon's crocodile head. My foot hits it just beneath the tip of its snout. Vein's head snaps back and she tumbles away with a grunt.

I don't stop to check on Artery. I burst through to the kitchen and throw myself at the door. My fingers tighten on the handle. I twist — the wrong way! Reverse the movement. A click. The door opens . . .

. . . and slams shut again as Artery rams it. The force of the demon banging into the door knocks me aside. I roll out of harm's immediate way. When I sit up, Artery has recovered and is standing in front of the door, legs and arms spread, three sets of teeth glinting in the glow of the red light cast by the fire of his eyeless sockets.

I back away on my knees from the green-skinned hellchild. Stop — growling to my rear. A panicked glance. Vein closing in, blocking my retreat.

I'm caught between them.

Artery's smiling. He knows I'm finished. A cockroach topples from his head, lands on its back, rights itself. It starts to scuttle away. Artery steps on the roach and crushes it. Holds his foot up to me, so that I can see the insect's smeared remains. Laughs evilly.

A snapping sound behind me. The stench of blood and decay. Vein almost upon me. Artery hisses — he wants to join in the bloodshed, but he's wary. Won't desert his post. Better to stay and watch Vein kill me than go for the kill himself and leave the door unguarded. I sense the demon's fear of the one upstairs. He called these two his familiars — that means he's their master.

Vein butts me in the back with her leathery snout. Growls throatily. It's over. I'm finished. Dead, like Mom and Dad and . . .

"No!" I roar, startling the demons. My thoughts flash on the telephone smashing through the sturdy wood of the front door, and Artery and the speed with which he moved. My eyes fix on the dog flap. Much too small to fit through, but I don't think of that. I focus only on escape.

I bring my legs up. Come to a half-crouch. Propel myself at the dog flap as Vein snaps for me with her teeth. I fly through the air, faster than any human should or could. The fire in Artery's sockets flares with alarm. The demon snaps his tiny legs together. Too late! Before they close, I'm through, fingers pushing the dog flap up out of the way, arms, body and legs following. Shrieks and howls behind. But they can't harm me now. I'm flying . . . outside . . . *free!*

✠ Soaring. Arms spread like wings. Exhilaration. Magic. Momentary delight. I feel invincible, like a —

Smash!

The backyard fence cuts short my flight. I hit the ground hard. Come up groaning and wheezing. Right elbow cut where I rocketed off the rough wood of the fence. Woozy. I stagger to my feet. Feel sick.

I remember the demons. My eyes snap to the dog flap. I turn to run . . .

. . . then stop. No sign of them. Ordinary night silence. They aren't following.

I stare at the dog flap — tiny — then at my arms and legs. The three red ravines gouged out by Vein. My shirt and jeans ripped from where the demons snagged me. My left shoe missing — it must have come off mid-flight. But otherwise I'm unharmed.

No way! Even if the dog flap had been bigger, I couldn't have dived through it at that speed without scraping myself raw. How did . . . ?

All questions die unvoiced as I recall the horror show of the bedroom.

"Mom," I sob, staggering towards the back door. I pause with my hand on the handle. Almost turn it. Can't.

I get down on my knees. Cautiously poke open the dog flap. Peer into the kitchen. No demons — but the many bloody prints on the tiles are proof I didn't imagine the chase.

On my feet. Again I try to enter. Again I can't bring myself to do it. Memories too terrifying. The demons too threatening. If I could help my family, perhaps it would be different. But they're dead, all of them, and I have too much sense (or not enough courage) to risk my life for a trio of corpses.

Stepping back from the door, I stare up at the house. It looks like all the others from the outside. No webs. No blood. Normal walls and windows.

"Gret," I mutter mindlessly. "I never said sorry for the rat guts."

I think about that for a moment, stunned, sluggish. Then I raise my face, open my mouth, and scream.

It's a wordless scream. Pure hatred. Pure sorrow. It builds from somewhere deep within me and bursts forth with the same impossible force I summoned when lobbing the telephone at Artery and diving through the dog flap.

The glass in the windows shatters and explodes inwards, ripping curtains to shreds, littering floors with jagged, transparent shards. The glass in the houses to either side also explodes. And in the nearby cars and street lamps.

I scream as long as I can — perhaps a full minute without pause — then lapse into a silence as all-encompassing as the scream. It's an isolated silence. Almost solid. No sounds trickle out and none penetrate.

After a while people emerge from the neighboring houses, shaken, making their cautious way to the source of the insane howl. I see their mouths moving, but I don't hear their questions, or their cries when they enter my house and come racing out shortly after, faces white, eyes filled with terror.

I'm in a world of my own. A world of webs and blood. Demons and corpses. Nightmares and terror. The name of the world from this night on — *home.*

DERVISH

✠ ✠ ✠

Lost, spiraling time. Muddled happenings. Flitting in and out of reality. Momentarily here, then gone, reclaimed by madness and demons.

Clarity. A warm room. Police officers. I'm wrapped in blankets. A man with a kind face offers me a mug of hot chocolate. I take it. He's asking questions. His words sail over and through me. Staring into the dark liquid of the mug, I begin to fade out of reality. To avoid the return to nightmares, I lift my head and focus on his moving lips.

For a long time — nothing. Then whispers. They grow. Like turning up the volume on the TV. Not all his words make sense — there's a roaring sound inside my head — but I get his general drift. He's asking about the murders.

"Demons," I mutter, my first utterance since my soul-wrenching cry.

His face lights up and he snaps forward. More questions. Quicker than before. Louder. More urgent. Amidst the babble, I hear him ask, "Did you see them?"

"Yes," I croak. "Demons."

He frowns. Asks something else. I tune out. The world flames at the edges. A ball of madness condenses around me, trapping me, devouring me, cutting off all but the nightmares.

✛ A different room. Different officers. More demanding than the last one. Not as gentle. Asking questions loudly, facing me directly, holding my head up until our eyes meet and they have my attention. One holds up a photograph — red, a body torn down the middle.

"Gret," I moan.

"I know it's hard," an officer says, sympathy mixed with impatience, "but did you see who killed her?"

"Demons," I sigh.

"Demons don't exist, Grubbs," the officer growls. "You're old enough to know that. Look, I know it's hard," he repeats himself, "but you have to focus. You have to help us find the people who did this."

"You're our only witness, Grubbs," his colleague murmurs. "You saw them. Nobody else did. We know you don't want to think about it right now, but you have to. For your parents. For Gret."

The other cop waves the photo in my face again. "Give us something — anything!" he pleads. "How many were there? Did you see their faces or were they wearing masks? How much of it did you witness? Can you . . ."

Fading. Bye-bye officers. Hello horror.

✛ ✛ ✛

✠ Screaming. Deafening cries. Looking around, wondering who's making such a racket and why they aren't being silenced. Then I realize it's *me* screaming.

In a white room. Hands bound by a tight white jacket. I've never seen a real one before, but I know what it is — a straitjacket.

I focus on making the screams stop and they slowly die away to a whimper. I don't know how long I've been roaring, but my throat's dry and painful, as though I've been testing its limits for weeks without pause.

There's a hard plastic mug set in a holder on a small table to my left. A straw sticks out of it. I ease my lips around the head of the straw and swallow. Flat coke. It hurts going down, but after a couple of mouthfuls it's wonderful.

Refreshed, I study my cell. Padded walls. Dim lights. A steel door with a strong plastic panel in the upper half, instead of glass.

I stumble to the panel and stare out. Can't see much — the area beyond is dark, so the plastic's mostly reflective. I study my face in the makeshift mirror. My eyes aren't my own — bloodshot, wild, rimmed with black circles. Lips bitten to shreds. Scratches on my face — self-inflicted. Hair cut short, tighter than I'd like. A large purple bruise on my forehead.

A face pops up close on the other side of the glass. I fall backwards with fright. The door open and a large, smiling woman enters. "It's OK," she says softly. "My name's Leah. I've been looking after you."

"Wh-wh . . . where am I?" I gasp.

"Someplace safe," she replies. She bends and touches the bruise on my forehead with two soft, gentle fingers. "You've been through hell, but you're OK now. It's all uphill from here. Now that you've snapped out of your delirium, we can work on . . ."

I lose track of what Leah's saying. Behind her, in the doorway, I imagine a pair of demons — Vein and Artery. The sane part of me knows they aren't real, just visions, but that part of me has no control over my senses anymore. Backing up against one of the padded walls, I stare blankly at the make-believe demons as they dance around my cell, making crude gestures and mimed threats.

Leah goes on talking. The imaginary Vein and Artery go on dancing. I slip back into the shell of my nightmares — almost gratefully.

✠ In and out. Quiet moments of reality. Sudden flashes of insanity and terror.

I'm being held in an institute for people with problems — that's all any of my nurses will tell me. No names. No mingling with the other patients. White rooms. Nurses — Leah, Kelly, Tim, Aleta, Emilia, and others, all nice, all concerned, all unable to coax me back from my nightmares when they strike. Doctors with names that I don't bother memorizing. They examine me at regular intervals. Make notes. Ask questions.

"What did you see?"

"What did the killers look like?"

"Why do you insist on calling them demons?"

"You know demons aren't real. Who are the real killers?"

One of them asks if *I* committed the murders. She's a grey-haired, sharp-eyed woman. Not as kindly as the rest. The "bad doctor" to their "good doctors." She presses me harder as the days slip by. Challenges me. Shows me photos that make me cry.

I start calling her Doctor Slaughter, but only to myself, not out loud. When she comes with her questions and cold eyes, I open myself to the nightmares — always hovering on the edges, eager to embrace me — and lose myself to the real world. After a few of these intentional fadeouts, they obviously decide to abandon the shock tactics, and that's the last I see of Doctor Slaughter.

✚ Time dragging or disappearing into nightmares. No ordinary time. No lazy afternoons or quiet mornings. The murders impossible to forget. Grief and fear tainting my every waking and sleeping moment.

Routines are important, according to my doctors and nurses, who wish to put a stop to my nightmarish withdrawals. They're trying to get me back to real time. They surround me with clocks. Make me wear two watches. Stress the times at which I'm to eat and bathe, exercise and sleep.

Lots of pills and injections. Leah says it's only temporary, to calm me down. Says they don't like dosing patients here. They prefer to talk us through our problems, not make us forget them.

The drugs numb me to the nightmares, but also to everything else. Impossible to feel interest or boredom, excitement or despair. I wander around the hospital — I have a free run now that I'm no longer violent — in a daze, zom-biefied, staring at clock faces, counting the seconds until my next pill.

✠ Off the pills. Coming down hard. Screaming fits. Fighting the nurses. Craving numbness. Needing pills!

They ignore my screams and pleas. Leah explains what's happening. I'm on a long-term treatment plan. The drugs put a stop to the nightmares and anchored me in the real world — step one. Now I have to learn to function in it as a normal person, free of medicinal depressants — step two.

I try explaining my situation to her — my nightmares won't ever go away, because the demons I saw were *real* — but she refuses to listen. Nobody believes me when I talk about the demons. They accept that I was in the house at the time of the murders, and that I witnessed something dread-ful, but they can't see beyond human horrors. They think I imagined the demons to mask the truth. One doctor says it's easier to believe in demons than evil humans. Says a wicked person is far scarier than a fanciful demon.

Moron. He wouldn't say that if he'd seen the crocodile-headed Vein or the cockroach-crowned Artery!

✠ Gradual improvement. I lose my craving for drugs, and no longer throw fits. But I don't progress as quickly as my doc-tors anticipated. I keep slipping back into the world of night-mares, losing my grip on reality. I don't talk openly with my nurses and doctors. I don't discuss my fears and pains. Some-times I babble incoherently and can't interpret the words of those around me. Or I'll stand staring at a tree or bush through one of the institute windows all day long, or not get up in the morning, despite the best rousing efforts of my nurses. I'm fighting them. They don't believe my story, so they can't truly understand me, so they can't really help me. So I fight them. Out of fear and spite.

✠ Somewhere in the middle of the confusion, relatives arrive. The doctors want me to focus on the world outside this institute. They think the way to do that is to reintroduce me to my family, break down my sense of overwhelming isolation. I think the plan is for the visitors to fuss over me, so that I want to be with them, so I'll then play ball with the doctors when they start in with the questions.

Aunt Kate's the first. She clutches me tight and weeps. Talks about Mom, Dad, and Gret nonstop, recalling all the good times that she can remember. Begs me to let the doctors help me, to talk with them, so I can get better and go home and live with her. I say nothing, just stare off into space and think about Dad hanging upside down. Aunt Kate leaves less than an hour later, still sobbing.

More relatives drop in during the following days and weeks, rounded up by the doctors. Aunts, uncles, cousins — both sides of the family tree. Some are old acquaintances. Some I've never seen before. I don't respond to any of them. I can tell they're just like the doctors. They don't believe me.

Lots of questions from my carers. Why don't I talk to my relatives? Do I like them? Are there others I prefer? Am I afraid of people? How would I feel about leaving here and staying with one of the well-wishers for a while?

They're trying to ship me out. It's not that they're sick of me — just step three on my path to recovery. Since I won't rally to their calls in here, they hope that a taste of the real world will make me more receptive. (I haven't developed any great insights into the human way of thinking — I know all this because Leah and the other nurses tell me. They say it's good for me to know what they're thinking, what their plans are.)

I do my best to give them what they want — I'd love if they could cure me — but it's difficult. The relatives remind me of what happened. They can't act naturally around me. They look at me with pitying — sometimes fearful — expressions. But I try. I listen. I respond.

✚ After much preparation and discussions, I spend a weekend with Uncle Mike and his family. Mike is Mom's younger brother. He has a pretty wife — Rosetta — and three children, two girls and a boy. Gret and I stayed with them a few times in the past, when Mom and Dad were away on vacation.

They try hard to make me feel welcome. Conor — Mike's son — is ten years old. He shows me his toys and plays computer games with me. He's bright and friendly. Talks me through his comics collection and tells me I can pick out any three issues I like and keep them.

The girls — Lisa and Laura — are seven and six. Gigglish. Not sure why I'm here or aware of what happened to me. But they're nice. They tell me about school and their friends. They want to know if I have a girlfriend.

Saturday goes well. I feel Mike's optimism — he thinks

this will work, that I'll return to my senses and pick up my life as normal. I try to believe salvation can come that simply, but inside I know I'm deluding myself.

✣ Sunday. A stroll in the park. Playing with Lisa and Laura on the swings. Pushing them high. Rosetta close by, keeping a watchful eye on me. Mike on the merry-go-round with Conor.

"Want off!" Laura shouts. I stop her and she hops to the ground. "Look what I saw!" she yells gleefully, and rushes over to a bush at the side of the swings. I follow. She points to a dead bird — small, young, its body ripped apart, probably by a cat.

"Cool!" Lisa gasps, coming up behind.

"No, it's not," Rosetta says, wandering over. "It's sad."

"Can we take it home and bury it?" Lisa asks.

"I don't know," Rosetta frowns. "It looks like it's been —"

"Demons killed my parents and sister," I interrupt calmly. The girls stare at me with round, wide eyes. "One of them ripped my Dad's head clean off. Blood was pouring out. Like from a faucet."

"Grubitsch, I don't think —" Rosetta says.

"One of the demons had the body of a child," I continue, unable to stop. "It had green skin and no eyes. Instead of hair, its head was covered with cockroaches."

"That's enough!" Rosetta snaps. "You're terrifying the girls. I won't —"

"The cockroaches were alive. They were eating the demon's flesh. If I'd looked closely enough, I'm sure I'd have seen its brains."

Rosetta storms off, Lisa and Laura in tow. Laura's crying.

I gaze sadly at the dead bird. Nightmares gather around me. Imagined demonic chuckles. The last thing I see in the real world — Mike marching towards me, torn between concern and fury.

✠ The institute. Days — weeks? months? — later. Lots of questions.

"Why did you say that to the girls?"

"Do you want to hurt other people?"

"Are you angry? Sad? Scared?"

"Would you like to visit somebody else?"

I don't answer, or else I grunt in response. They don't understand. They can't. I didn't want to scare Lisa or Laura, or upset Mike and Rosetta. The words came out by themselves. The doctors can't help. If I had an ordinary illness, I'm sure they could fix me. But I've seen demons rip my world to pieces. Nobody believes that, so nobody knows what I'm going through. I'm alone. I always will be. That's my life now. That's just the way it is.

✠ The relatives stop coming. The doctors stop trying. They say they're giving me time to recover, but I think they just don't know how to handle me. Long periods by myself, walking, reading, thinking. Tired most of the time. Headaches. Imaginary demons everywhere I look. Hard to keep food down. Growing thin. Sickly.

The nurses try to rally my spirits. Days out — a circus, amusement park, cinemas — and parties in my cell. No good. Their efforts are wasted on me. I draw into myself more and more. Hardly ever speak. Avoid eye contact. Fingers twitch and head twists with fear at the slightest alien sound.

Getting worse. Going downhill.

There's talk of new pills.

✠ A visitor. It's been a long time since the last. I thought they'd given up.

It's Uncle Dervish. Dad's younger brother. I don't know much about him. A man of mystery. He visited us a few times when I was smaller. Mom never liked him. I recall her and Dad arguing about him once. "We're not taking the kids there!" she snapped. "I don't trust him."

Leah admits Uncle Dervish. Asks if he'd like anything to drink or eat. "No, thanks." Would *I* like anything? I shake my head. Leah leaves.

Dervish Grady is a thin, lanky man. Bald on top, grey hair at the sides, a tight grey beard. Pale blue eyes. I remember his eyes from when I was a kid. I thought they looked like my toy soldier's eyes. I asked him if he was in the army. He laughed.

He's dressed completely in denim — jeans, shirt, jacket. He looks ridiculous — Gret used to say denim looks dumb on anyone over the age of thirty. She was right.

Dervish sits in the visitor's chair and studies me with cool, serious eyes. He's immediately different from all who've come before. Whereas the other relatives were quick to start a false, cheerful conversation, or cry, or say how sorry they were, Dervish just sits and stares. That interests me, so I stare back, more alert than I've been in weeks.

"Hello," I say after a full minute of silence.

Dervish nods in reply.

I try thinking of a follow-up line. Nothing comes to mind.

Dervish looks slowly around the room. Stands, walks to the window, gazes out at the rear yard of the institute, then swings back to the door, which Leah left ajar. He pokes his head out, looks left and right. Closes the door. Returns to the chair and sits. Unbuttons the top of his denim jacket. Slides out three sheets of paper. Holds them facedown.

I sit upright, intrigued but suspicious. Is this some new ploy of the doctors? Have they fed Dervish a fresh set of lines and actions, in an attempt to spark my revival?

"I hope this isn't a Rorschach test." I grin weakly. "I've had enough inkblots to last me a —"

Dervish turns a sheet over and I stop dead. It's a black-and-white drawing of a large dog with a crocodile's head and human hands.

"Vein," Dervish says. He has a soft, lyrical voice.

I tremble and say nothing in reply.

He turns over the second sheet. Color this time. A child with green skin. Mouths in its palms. Fire in its eyes. Lice for hair.

"Artery," Dervish says.

"You got the hair wrong," I mumble. "It should be cock-roaches."

"Lice, cockroaches, leeches — it changes," he says, and lays the two sheets down on the floor. He turns over the third. This one's color too. A thin man, lumpy red skin, large red eyes, mangled hands, no feet, a snake-filled hole where his heart should be.

"The doctors put you up to this," I moan, averting my

eyes. "I told them about the demons. They must have got artists to draw them. Why are you —"

"You didn't tell them *his* name," Dervish cuts me short. He taps the picture. "You said the other two were familiars, and this one was their master — but you never mentioned his name. Do you know it?"

I think back to those few minutes of insanity in my parents' bedroom. The demon lord didn't say much. Never told me who he was. I open my mouth to answer negatively . . .

. . . then slowly let it close. No — he *did* reveal his identity. I can't remember when, exactly, but somewhere among the madness there was mention of it. I cast my thoughts back. Zone in on the moment. It was when he asked if I knew why this was happening, if my parents had ever told me the story of —

"Lord Loss," Dervish says, a split second before I blurt it out.

I stare at him . . . uncertain . . . terrified . . . yet somehow excited.

"I know the demons were real," Dervish murmurs, picking up the pictures and placing them back inside his jacket, doing up his buttons. He stands. "If you want to come live with me, you can. But you'll have to sort out the mess you're in first. The doctors say you won't respond to their questions. They say they know how to help you, but that you won't let them."

"They don't believe me!" I cry. "How can they cure me when they think I'm lying about the demons?"

"The world's a confusing place," Dervish says. "I'm sure your parents told you to always tell the truth, and most of the time that's good advice. But sometimes you have to lie." He comes over and bends, so his face is in mine. "These people want to help you, Grubitsch. And I believe they can. But you're going to have to help them. You'll have to lie, pretend demons don't exist, tell them what they want to hear. You have to give a little to get a little. Once you remove that barrier, they can go to work on fixing your brain, on helping you deal with the grief. Then, when they've done all they can, you can come to me — if that's what you want — and I'll help you with the rest. I can explain about demons. And tell you why your parents and sister died."

He leaves.

✤ Stunned silence. Long days and nights of heavy thinking. Repeating the name of the thin red demon. Lord Loss, Lord Loss, Lord Loss, Lord . . .

Torn between hope and fear. Could Dervish be in league with the demons? Mom saying, "I don't trust him." I'm safe here. Leaving might be an invitation to danger and further sorrow. I won't improve in this place, holding true to my story, defying the doctors and nurses — but I can't be harmed either. Out in the real world, I might have to face demons again. Simpler to stay here and hide.

✤ One morning I wake from a nightmare. In it, I was at a party, wearing a mask. When I took the mask off, I realized I'd been wearing Gret's face.

Sitting up in bed. Shaking. Crying. I stare out the window at the world beyond.

I decide.

✠ ✠ ✠

✠ Exercising. Eating sensibly. Putting on weight. Talking directly with my doctors and nurses, answering their questions, letting them into my head, "baring my soul." I allow them to help me. I work with them. Lie when I have to. Say I saw humans in the room that night. Police come and take my statement. An artist captures my new, realistic, invented impressions of the murderers. My doctors beam proudly and pat my back.

Weeks pass. With help and lots of hard work, I get better. Dervish was right. Now that I'm working with them, they *are* able to help me, even if we're progressing on the basis of a lie — that demons aren't real. I weep a lot and learn a lot — how to face my grief, how to confront my fear and control it — and let them guide me out of the darkness, slowly, painfully, but surely.

In one afternoon session with a therapist, when I judge the time to be right, I make a request. Lots of discussions afterwards. Long debates. Staff meetings. Phone calls. Humming and hawing. Finally they agree. There's a big build-up. Lots of in-depth therapy sessions and heart-to-hearts. Tests galore, to make sure I'm ready, to reassure themselves that they're doing the right thing. They have doubts. They voice them. We talk them through. They decide in my favor.

The last day. Handshakes and emergency contact numbers from the doctors in case anything goes wrong. Kisses and hugs from my favorite nurses. A card from Leah. Facing the door, a bag on my shoulder with all I have left in the world. Scared sick but determined to see it through.

I leave the institute on the back of a motorbike. Driving — my rescuer, my lifeline, my hope — Uncle Dervish.

"Hold on tight," he says. "Speed limits were made to be broken."

Vroom!

THE GRAND TOUR

✠   ✠   ✠

DERVISH drives like a madman, a hundred miles an hour. Howling wind. Blurred countryside. No chance to talk or study the scenery. I spend the journey with my face pressed between my uncle's shoulder blades, clinging on for dear life.

Finally, coming to a small village, he slows. I peek and catch the name on a sign as we exit — Carcery Vale.

"Carkerry Vale," I murmur.

"It's pronounced Car-sherry," Dervish grunts.

"This is where you live," I note, recalling the address from cards I wrote and sent with Mom and Gret. (Mom didn't like Uncle Dervish but she always sent him a Christmas and birthday card.)

"Actually, I live about two miles beyond," Dervish says, carefully overtaking a tractor and waving to the driver. "It's pretty lonely out where I am, but there are lots of kids in the village. You can walk in any time you like."

"Do they know about me?" I ask.

"Only that you're an orphan and you're coming to live with me."

A winding road. Lots of potholes that Dervish swerves expertly to avoid. The sides of the road are lined with trees. They grow close together, blocking out all but the thinnest slivers of sunlight. Dark and cold. I press closer to Dervish, hugging warmth from him.

"The trees don't stretch back very far," he says. "You can skirt around them when you're going to the village."

"I'm not afraid," I mutter.

"Of course you are," he chuckles, then looks back quickly. "But you have my word — you've no need to be."

✠ *Chez* Dervish. Three storeys. Three floors. Built from rough white blocks, almost as big as those I've seen in photos of the pyramids. Shaped like an L. The bit sticking out at the end is made from ordinary red bricks and doesn't look like the rest of the house. Lots of timber decorations around the top and down the sides. A slate roof with three enormous chimneys. The roof on the brick section is flat and the chimney's tiny in comparison with the others. The windows on the lower floor run from the ground to the ceiling. The windows on the upper floors are smaller, round, and feature stained-glass designs. On the brick section they're very ordinary.

"It's not much," Dervish says wryly, "but it's home."

"This place must have cost a fortune!" I gasp, standing close to the motorbike, staring at the house, almost afraid to venture any nearer.

"Not really," Dervish says. "It was a wreck when I bought it.

No roof or windows, the interior destroyed by exposure to the elements. The lower floor was used by a local farmer to house pigs. I lived in the brick extension for years while I restored the main building. I keep meaning to tear the extension down — I don't use it anymore, and it takes away from the the main structure — but I never seem to get around to it."

Dervish removes his helmet, helps me out of mine, then walks me around the outside of the house. He explains about the original architect and how much work he had to do to make the house habitable again, but I don't listen very closely. I'm too busy assessing the mansion and the surrounding terrain — lots of open fields, sheep and cattle in some of them, a small forest to the west that runs all the way to Carcery Vale, no neighboring houses that I can see.

"Do you live here alone?" I ask as we return to the front of the house.

"Pretty much," Dervish says. "One farmer owns most of this land, and he's opposed to over-development. He's old. I guess his children will sell plots off when he dies. But for the last twenty years I've had all the peace and seclusion a man could wish for."

"Doesn't it get lonely?" I ask.

"No," Dervish says. "I'm fairly solitary by nature. When I'm in need of company, it's only a short stroll to the village. And I travel a lot — I have many friends around the globe."

We stop at the giant front doors, a pair of them, like the entrance to a castle. No doorbell — just two chunky gargoyle-shaped knockers, which I eye apprehensively.

Dervish doesn't open the doors. He's studying me quietly.

"Have you lost the key?" I ask.

"We don't have to enter," he says. "I think you'll grow to love this place after a while, but it's a lot to take in at the start. If you'd prefer, you could stay in the brick extension — it's an eyesore, but cozy inside. Or we can drive to the Vale and you can spend a few nights in a B&B until you get your bearings."

It's tempting. If the house is even half as spooky on the inside as it looks from out here, it's going to be hard to adapt to. But if I don't move in now, I'm sure the house will grow far creepier in my imagination than it can ever be in real life.

"Come on." I grin weakly, lifting one of the gargoyle knockers and rapping loudly. "We look like a pair of idiots, standing out here. Let's go in."

✛ Cold inside but brightly lit. No carpets — all tiles or stone floors — but many rugs and mats. No wallpaper — some of the walls are painted, others just natural stone. Chandeliers in the main hall and dining room. Wall-set lamps in the other rooms.

Bookcases everywhere, most of them filled. Chess boards too, in every room — Dervish must be as keen on chess as Mom and Dad. Ancient weapons hang from many of the walls — swords, axes, maces.

"For when the tax collector calls," Dervish says solemnly, lifting down one of the larger swords. He swings it over his head and laughs.

"Can I try it?" I ask. He hands it to me. "Hell!" It's *H-E-A V-Y*. I can lift it to thigh level but no higher. A quick reappraisal of Uncle Dervish — he looks wiry as a rat, but he must have hidden muscles under all the denim.

We meander through the downstairs rooms, Dervish explaining what each was used for in the past, pointing out items of special interest, such as a stuffed bear's head that is more than two hundred years old, a cage where a live vulture was kept, rusty nails that were used by the Romans to crucify people.

There's a large, empty fish tank in one of the main living rooms, set against a wall. Dervish pauses at it and taps the frame with his fingernails. "The last owner of this place — before it fell into ruin — was a tyrant called Lord Sheftree. He kept live piranhas in this tank. One day, a woman turned up with a baby — she claimed it was his, and she wanted money to pay for its upkeep."

Dervish crouches down and stares into the abandoned aquarium, as though it's still full of circling, multicolored fish.

"Lord Sheftree invited her to stay for the night," he says calmly. "While she was sleeping, he crept into her room and removed her baby. Brought it down here and fed it to the piranhas. Took the bones away and buried them. The woman raised almighty hell, but search parties couldn't find a corpse, and nobody had seen her arrive with a child — so there was no proof she ever had one. She ranted and raved and was eventually locked away in a mental asylum. She hanged herself there.

"Years later, when Lord Sheftree was an old man and his mind was wandering, he boasted about the murder to one of his servants, and told her where the bones were buried. She dug them up and informed the police. They came to arrest him, but the local villagers got here first. He was discovered chopped up into tiny pieces — all of which had been dropped into the piranha tank."

Dervish stops and I gaze at him in silent awe.

He stands and faces me. "I'm not saying this to scare you," he smiles, "but this house has a long and bloody history. There are dozens of horror stories, none quite as gruesome as that one, but all of them pretty gut-churning. I think it's best you hear about its past now, from me."

"Is . . . is the house haunted?" I wheeze.

"No," he answers seriously. "It's safe. I wouldn't have brought you here if it wasn't. If the nightmares of the past prove too oppressive, you're free to leave. But you've nothing to fear in the present."

I nod slowly, thinking about Lord Sheftree and his piranha, wondering if I have the courage to spend the night in a house like this.

"Are you OK?" Dervish asks. "Would you like to step outside for fresh air?"

"I'm fine," I mutter, turning my back on the fish tank, acting like I hear this sort of stuff all the time. "What's upstairs?"

✠ Mostly bedrooms on the first floor. All are fully fitted, the beds freshly made, though Dervish says only four or five of the rooms have been used since he renovated the mansion.

"Why bother with all the beds then?" I ask.

"If something's worth doing, it's worth doing right," he laughs.

Some of the beds are four-posters, imported from foreign countries, with histories as old and macabre as the house. It's only when Dervish is telling me about one particular bed, in which a French aristocrat hid for four months during the Revolution, that I think about how much they must have cost.

"What do you *do*?" I ask my uncle. It sounds ridiculous, but I don't recall Mom or Dad ever mentioning Dervish's line of work.

"I dabble in antiques," he says. "Rare books are my speciality — particularly books regarding the occult."

Dervish looks at me questioningly — we haven't mentioned demons since he picked me up at the institute. He's offering me the chance to quiz him about them now. But I'm not ready to discuss Lord Loss or his minions yet.

"You must be good at it, to afford a place like this," I say, sliding away from the larger questions and issues.

"It's a hobby," he demurs, leading me down a long corridor full of framed portraits and photographs. "The money's good, but I don't worry too much about it."

"Then how do you pay for all this?" I ask nosily.

Dervish quickens his pace. I think he's avoiding the question, but then he stops at one of the older portraits and points at it. "Recognize him?"

I study the face of an old man — lined, quite a large nose, but otherwise unspectacular. "Is he famous?" I ask.

"Only to us," Dervish says. "He was your great-great-great-grandfather. Bartholomew Garadex. That's our original family name, on our paternal side — it got shortened to Grady around your great-grandfather's time." He points to a nearby portrait. "That's him." Waving a hand at the hall in general, he adds, "They're all part of our family. Garadexes, Gradys, Bells, Moores — if one of our relations has been photographed or painted, you'll most probably find them here."

Returning to the portrait of my great-great-great-grandfather, he says, "Bartholomew was a sublimely clever man.

He started with nothing but had amassed a fortune by the time of his death. We're still living off of it — at least, *I* am. Cal preferred to make his own way in the world, and only dipped into the family coffers in emergencies."

"How much is left?" I inquire.

"Quite a lot," Dervish says vaguely. "Your great-great-grandfather — one of old Bart's boys — wasted most of it. Then his son — the one who changed the family name — restored it. It's been fairly constant since, much of it tied up in bonds and properties that yield steady profits."

"Who does it go to when . . ." I stop and blush. "I mean, who's your heir?"

Dervish doesn't answer immediately. He gazes at the face in the portrait, as though seeing it for the first time. Then he looks away and says quietly, "I have no children. I've willed portions of the estate to various friends and causes. I always meant for the majority of my assets to go to Cal and his kids. Since you're the only survivor . . ."

My stomach tightens — Dervish sounds as if he's accusing me of caring more about money than my family. "I'd swap any amount of a fortune if I could bring Mom and Dad and Gret back," I snarl defensively.

"Of course you would." Dervish frowns, glancing at me oddly, and I realize I was only imagining the accusation.

"Let's go," Dervish says. "There's another floor to explore — and a cellar."

"A cellar?" I ask nervously.

"Yes," he says. "That's where I bury the bodies."

I freeze, and he has to stop and wink broadly before I catch the joke.

✠ ✠ ✠

✠ Lots of storage space on the second floor — rooms packed with crates, statues, and boxes of books. There are a couple of small bedrooms, including Dervish's, and the centerpiece — his study.

Unlike every other room in the mansion, Dervish's study is carpeted and the walls are covered with leather panels. It's a colossal room, the size of seven or eight of the bedrooms, with two desks larger than most of the beds I've seen. There are bookcases, on which small numbers of books are carefully arranged. He has a PC, a laptop, a typewriter, several writing pads, and a multitude of pens. There are five chess sets in the room, each different, one made entirely of crystal, another with solid gold pieces. A sword and axe hang from each wall, their handles encrusted with precious jewels, their blades gleaming brightly.

"This is wild." I grin, circling the study, checking out some of the book titles — all to do with ghosts, werewolves, magic, and other occult-related items.

"Some of my rarer finds," Dervish says, picking up a book and smiling as he flicks through it. "The great thing about having loads of money is not having to sell to survive."

"Aren't you afraid of burglars?" I ask. "Wouldn't this stuff be safer in a museum?"

"The contents of this room are protected," he says. "Anyone breaking in is free to plunder the rest of the house as they please — but they won't take anything from here."

"What sort of security system do you use?" I ask. "Lasers? Heat sensors?"

"Magic."

I start to smirk, thinking this is another of his jokes, but his grim expression unnerves me.

"I've cast some of my strongest spells on this room," he says. "Anybody who enters without my permission will run into serious obstacles. And I don't use that phrase lightly."

Dervish sits in the large leather chair behind one of the desks and rocks lightly to the left and right as he addresses me. "I know there's nothing as tempting as forbidden fruit, Grubitsch, but I've got to ask you not to come into this room when I'm not here. There are spells I can cast to protect you — and spells I can teach you when you're ready to learn — but it's safest not to tempt fate."

"Are you . . ." I have to wet my lips to continue. "Are you a magician?"

"No," he chuckles. "But I know many of the ways of magic. Bartholomew Garadex was a magician — among other things — but there hasn't been one in the family since. Real magicians are rare. You can't become one — you have to be born to it. Ordinary people like you and me can study magic and make it work to an extent, but true magicians have the natural power to change the shape of the world with a click of their fingers. It wouldn't do to have too many people with that kind of power walking around. Nature limits us to one or two per century."

"Is . . ." I hate to say his name out loud, but I must. "Is Lord Loss a magician?"

Dervish's eyes are dark. "No. He's a demon master. He's as far advanced of magicians as magicians are of the rest of us."

"When I . . . was escaping . . . I used magic."

"To fit through the dog flap." He nods. "Many of us have magical potential. It usually lies dormant, but the presence of the demons enabled you to tap into yours. The magic within you reacted to theirs. Without it, you would have died, along with the others."

I stare wordlessly at Uncle Dervish. He speaks so honestly, so matter-of-factly, that he could be explaining a math problem. There's so much I want to ask, so many questions. But this isn't the time. I'm not ready.

I scratch my head and pluck a long ginger hair from behind my left ear. I rub it between my fingers until it falls, then face Dervish and grin shakily. "I'll agree to stay out of your study if you'll do something for me in return."

"What?" he asks, and I can tell he's expecting an overbearing request.

"Will you call me 'Grubbs'? I can't stand 'Grubitsch.'"

✠ The cellar's full of wine racks and dusty bottles.

"My other great love, apart from books," Dervish purrs, wiping clean the label of a large green bottle. He advances, lights flicking on ahead of him as he walks. I wonder if it's magic, until I spot motion-detection sensors overhead.

"Do you drink wine?" he asks, leading me down one of the many rack-lined aisles of the cellar.

"Mom and Dad let us have a glass with dinner sometimes, but I don't really like it," I answer.

"Shocking!" he tuts. "I'll have to educate your palate. Wine is as varied and unpredictable as people. There are some vintages you just won't get along with, no matter how famous or popular they are, but you'll always find something you like — if you search hard enough."

He stops, picks out another bottle, appraises and replaces it. "I roam around for hours down here some days," he sighs. "Half the pleasure of having such a fine collection is forgetting what's here and rediscovering it by accident years later. The choosing of a bottle can be almost as much fun as the drinking of it." He snorts. "*Almost!*"

We return to the steps leading up to the kitchen and he pauses. "I have to ask you not to come down here either," he says. "But this has nothing to do with spells or magic. The temperature and humidity have to be maintained *just so.*" He pinches his left thumb and index finger together. "I'm fairly easygoing when it comes to material possessions, but where my wine's concerned I'm unbelievably cranky. If you caused an accident . . ." He shook his head glumly. "I wouldn't say much, but I'd silently despise you forever."

"I'll steer clear," I laugh. "I'll find a different source if I want to go boozing."

Dervish smiles and leads the way up. The lights switch off automatically behind us, plunging the cellar into cool, precision gloom.

✠ "And that's it."

Back where we started, the main hall, beneath the giant chandelier. Dervish checks his watch. "I usually have dinner anywhere between five and seven. You can eat with me — I'm a nifty little chef, if I do say so myself — or do your own cooking and eat whenever you like. The freezer's stocked with pizzas and microwave dinners."

"I'll eat with you," I tell him.

"Then I'll shout when it's ready. In the meantime, feel free to explore, either inside or out. And remember — you can't come to any harm here."

He heads for the wide set of marble stairs leading to the first and second floors.

"Wait!" I stop him. "You never showed me my room."

Dervish slaps his forehead playfully. "You'll get used to that," he chuckles. "I'm forever overlooking the obvious. Well, there are fourteen bedrooms to choose from — any except mine is yours for the taking."

"You don't have a room set aside for me?" I ask, surprised.

"I thought about it," he replies, "but I decided to let you choose for yourself. You can test out as many as you like. If you want to stay on the upper floor, close to me, you can — though the rooms there are quite modest compared to those on the first floor."

He tips an imaginary hat to me, then trots up the stairs to his study.

Standing alone in the vast hall. The house creaks around me. I shiver, then recall Uncle Dervish's promise — I can't come to any harm here. I shake off the creeps before they have a chance to take hold.

Picking up my bag, which I dropped by the front doors when we came in, I climb the ornate stairs and go searching among the beautifully kept, expansive array of rooms for one that I can dump my gear in and call my own.

PORTRAITS

✠　　✠　　✠

I DON'T expect to get much sleep the first night — new surroundings, new bed, new life — but surprisingly I drop off within minutes of climbing underneath the covers of the small first-floor bed I chose, and don't wake until close to ten in the morning.

I feel good as I use the *en suite* bathroom. Refreshed. The sun's broken through the clouds and is shining directly onto my bed when I come out of the bathroom. I lie on the covers and bask in the rays, smiling softly. For a moment I think of Gret's *en suite* . . . the rat guts . . . the start of the nightmares. But I'm in too good a mood to dwell on all that. Shaking my thoughts free, I head downstairs for a late breakfast.

I'm finishing off my cornflakes and munching my third slice of toast when Dervish enters through the back door. He's been jogging. Red-faced, sweaty, panting.

"I looked in . . . on you . . . earlier," he gasps, rolling his neck around, jiggling his arms and legs. "Didn't have the heart . . . to wake you."

"I don't normally sleep this late." I grin guiltily.

"I should hope not." He stretches, holds his hands over his head while he counts to ten, then relaxes, pulls up a chair, and sits. "Any plans for today?"

"I'm not sure," I admit nervously. "I'm used to having nurses plan my days for me."

"I've been thinking about school," Dervish says. "Ideally I'd like to get you started quickly, but they're midway through the semester. You'd be playing catch-up from the second you sat down. I think it'd be easier if we waited until after the summer, when you can go in fresh with the rest of the class."

"OK." I'm relieved — I was dreading the return to school.

"If you want, I can give you some lessons, or we can enroll you for private tutoring," Dervish continues. "You've missed a lot, and I suspect you'll have to repeat a year, but if you work hard over the summer . . ."

"I'm not worried about repeating," I mutter. "If I was at my old school, I'd want to move up with my friends. But since I'm starting fresh, it doesn't really matter which class I go into."

"I like the way you think." Dervish smiles. "OK, we'll lay off the heavy grind, but fit the odd bit of learning in along the way — you'll get rusty if you don't keep your brain sharp."

"What about today?" I ask. "What should I do?"

"Get the lay of the land," Dervish suggests. "Explore the house. Have a look round the grounds and neighboring fields — you won't get in trouble for trespassing as long as you don't mess with the livestock. Maybe take a stroll to the village and let the gossips have a gawk — I'm sure they're dying to check out the new boy. You can start on the household chores tomorrow."

"Chores?"

"Sweeping, cleaning, stuff like that."

"Oh." I glance around. "I thought . . . a place this big . . . you'd have a maid or something."

"No maid!" Dervish laughs. "I have a woman who comes in every other week to dust the bedrooms, but that's it as far as outside help goes. You'll have to earn your keep here, Grubbs m'boy! But we'll start with the slave labor tomorrow, like I said. Find your feet first. Take it easy. Enjoy." He rises and his expression saddens. "Hell, you're due some enjoyment after all you've been through."

✠ I do the village first. Carcery Vale is quaint, quiet, picturesque. Nice white or creamy houses, smiling people, the occasional car puttering down the main street. I walk through the village, familiarizing myself with the layout. I pass the school — larger than I thought. It's lunch and the students are in the yard, shouting, laughing, playing football. I don't get close. Nervous. I've had months of dealing strictly with adults. I've almost forgotten what people my own age are like and how to get along with them.

Not many shops, and a very limited selection of goods. I need new clothes, but socks and underpants are all the local stores have to offer. I suppose there's a town within easy driving distance where Dervish can take me. I'll ask when I get back.

The people in the shops and on the streets eye me

curiously but without suspicion. I keep expecting them to ask for my name or pass a comment — "You must be Mr. Grady's new house guest," or "You're not from around here, are you?" — but they just nod pleasantly and let me go about my business.

✠ Early afternoon. Wandering around the mansion. Checking out the rooms.

I knew the instant I arrived that this was a monster of a house, but it's only today that I realize just how enormous it is. It doesn't have a single modest inch or nook to it. Everything's overblown and over-the-top. I feel out of place. I'm used to ordinary houses, wallpaper from chain stores, furniture bought from glossy catalogues, paperback bestsellers, and brand-name reference guides on the bookshelves.

But as awkward as I feel in this massive, ornate old house, I'm not scared. Although it reeks of history, and is full of barbaric weapons and grotesque items like the piranha tank, I'm not frightened. I don't get shivers down my spine strolling through the corridors (some longer than the street where I used to live). I don't imagine monsters lurking under the beds, or demons cackling in the shadows.

This house is safe. I'm protected within these walls. I don't know how I know — I just do.

✠ The hall of portraits. I've been here fifteen, maybe twenty minutes, studying the faces of my relatives. Most are strangers, faded faces from the long-forgotten past — many of them young, just teenagers — but some are familiar. I spot Grandad Grady, my great-aunt Martha, a few cousins I met when I was younger — all of whom have died during the course of my short life.

I look for my picture but I'm not among them. Dad and Gret are though, in new frames. Recent photos. I remember the day they were taken, last summer, when we were on vacation in Italy.

No photo of Mom. I go through them all again, but she isn't here. The two of us are missing.

✚ Shopping for clothes, twenty miles from Carcery Vale, in a large mall. Lots of people and noise. I feel lost in the crowd. Dervish sticks close by me, sensing my nervousness.

Kebabs when we've finished shopping. Hot and juicy. Dervish nibbles slowly at his, delicately. I finish long before him. Slurping down the last of my Coke. Studying him as he eats. Wondering if I should mention Mom's and my absence from the hall of portraits.

"An unasked question is the most futile thing in the world," Dervish says, startling me. Doesn't look up. Swallows his food. Waits.

"I was looking at the photos and portraits in the hall today," I begin.

"And you want to know why there are so many teenagers."

I frown. "No. I mean, I noticed that, but it was Mom and me I was curious about. You have photos of Dad and Gret, but not us."

"Oh." He grimaces. "My *faux pas*. Most people ask about the teens. The photos and portraits are all of dead family members. I like to frame them as they looked at the end of their lives, so most of the photos were taken shortly before the subject's death. We have a tragic family history — lots of us have been killed young — which is why there are so many pubescents up there."

He wipes around his mouth with a napkin, carefully balls it up, and lays it aside. "As for why Sharon hasn't been included, it's simple — no in-laws. Everybody on those walls is a blood relative. It's a family tradition. But I have lots of photos of her, as well as Cal and Gret, in albums that you're free to browse through."

"Maybe later," I smile. "I just wanted to make sure you didn't have any underhanded reasons for not including us with the others."

"Everything's aboveboard with me, Grubbs," Dervish says, then sips from his mug of coffee without taking his eyes off me. "Well — almost everything."

✠ Late. Close to midnight. In my pajamas. No slippers — I left my old pair at the hospital and I forgot to buy new ones today. The stone floor's cold. I have to keep moving my toes to keep them warm.

I'm drawn back to the hall of portraits. Studying them in moonlight, the faces mostly concealed by shadows. Focusing on the teenagers. Dozens of them, all my age or slightly older. Wondering why the faces of the dead teens fascinate me, and why I feel uneasy.

I'm back in my room, in bed, before the answer strikes and drives all hope of sleep away in a flash. In the restaurant, Dervish didn't simply say that many of our family members had died young — he said they'd been *killed*.

SPLEEN

✠　　✠　　✠

SETTLING in. Daily chores — washing up after meals, sweeping a different couple of floors each day, polishing the furniture in one of the large halls or rooms. Lots of other less-regular jobs — taking out the garbage, cleaning windows, running errands in the village.

I enjoy the work. It keeps me busy. Not much else to do here apart from play chess with Dervish, watch TV — Dervish has a massive 60-inch widescreen set, which he hardly ever uses! — and read. Chess doesn't thrill me — Dervish is like Mom and Dad, a chess fanatic, and beats me easily each time we play. I'd as soon not play at all, but he gently presses me to work on my game. I don't get my family's obsession with chess, but I guess I'll just have to bear it here like I did at home.

I read more than I normally do — I'm not big on *litrachoor* — but Dervish doesn't have a great collection of modern fiction. I pick up a few new books in the Vale, and order some more over the Internet, but I'm not spoiled for choice.

I try some of the thousands of occult books littering the shelves, figuring they've got to be better than watching the moon all night, but they're too complicated or densely written to be of interest.

So that leaves me with the TV — an endless stream of soap operas, talk shows, movies, sitcoms, sports programs. And while I never thought I'd admit such a thing, TV does get a bit boring after a while, if it's all you have to keep yourself amused.

But, hey, it's a million times better than the institute!

✠ A week passes. At ease with the house. Getting to know Dervish, though he's a hard one to figure. Kind, thoughtful, caring — but aloof, with a warped sense of humor. He came in one day while I was watching the news. Caught a report about a serial killer who'd chopped off and collected his victims' heads. Commented drily, "There's a man determined to get ahead in life." Spent the next five minutes doubled over with laughter, while I gazed at him, astonished, and the TV broadcast pictures of bloodbaths and weeping relatives.

His thirst for chess is at least equal to that of Dad and Mom, if not more so. He went easy on me to begin with, gently encouraging me to play, treating the games as fun. Now he's showing his true colors. Insists that I play with him every night and gets irritated when I play badly.

"You've got to love the game," he told me last night, tossing a captured rook at me with unexpected force. "Chess is life. You have to love it as you love living. If you don't . . ."

He said no more, just stormed out of the room, leaving me at a loss for words, rubbing my cheek where the rook struck. Later, when I'd recovered and was passing him in the hall on my way to bed, I muttered, "Get a life, you freak!" The perfect comeback — just an hour too late.

He's got no time for music. I find a grand total of three CDs in the house, all old albums by some group called Led Zeppelin. Doesn't read fiction. Watches only the occasional documentary on TV. Spends a lot of time on the Web, from what I've seen when I've visited him in his study. But he doesn't seem to surf or play games — he mostly exchanges e-mails with contacts around the globe, or visits dull-looking encylopedic sites.

Apart from his books and antiques, chess and jogging, and his e-mail friends, he doesn't seem to have any hobbies, or any apparent interest in the world beyond this house.

✠ There are stables — long abandoned — behind the mansion. I'm exploring one of them, idly toeing through the old nails and horseshoes on the ground in search of some interesting nugget, when somebody raps on the rotten door and startles me out of my skin.

"Peace, hombre," the stranger chuckles as I duck and grab a horseshoe for protection. "I come to greet you, not to eat you — as the cannibal said to the missionary."

A boy a year or so younger than me enters and sticks out his hand. I stare at it a moment, then shake it. He's a lot shorter than me, chubby, with black hair and a lazy left eye that hangs half-closed. Wearing a faded pair of jeans and an old Simpsons T-shirt.

"Bill-E Spleen," he says, pumping my hand. "And you're Grubbs 'don't call me Grubitsch!' Grady, right?"

"Right." I grin thinly, then repeat his name. "Billy Spleen?"

"Bill-E," he corrects me, and spells it out. "Actually, it's really Billy," he confesses, "but I changed it. I haven't been able to do it officially yet, but I will when I'm older. There's nothing wrong with Billy — it's a hell of a lot better than Grubitsch or Grubbs! — but Bill-E sounds cooler, like a rap star."

He talks quick and sharp, fingers dancing in the air to accent his words.

"Are you from the village?" I ask politely.

"Yup — I'm a Valer," he yawns, as though it's the dullest thing in the world. "I used to live a few miles over — in a cottage smaller than this stable — until Mom died. Then I moved in with my grandparents — 'the original Spleens,' as Mom used to call them. They're OK, just a bit old-fashioned and straitlaced."

Bill-E studies the disturbed nails and horseshoes on the ground and grins. "You won't find any gold here," he chortles. "I've been through these sheds more times than I can count, looking for old Lord Sheftree's treasure."

"Treasure?" Bill-E's a little too chummy for my liking — I've never been fond of people who come along and immediately start acting as though you're old friends — but I don't want to say anything to insult him, at least not until I know a bit more about him.

"You don't know about the treasure?" He hoots as though I've admitted I didn't know the world was round. "Lord Sheftree — he owned this place years ago — is supposed to have hidden cases full of treasure somewhere on these grounds. His getaway stash, in case he ever had to make a quick exit and needed some ready cash. He was a real swindler. He used to keep a fish tank full of —"

"— piranha," I interrupt. "And he fed a baby to them. I know."

"Dervish told you?" Bill-E looks disappointed. "I love telling that story. Just about everyone in Carcery Vale knows it, so it's not often that I have the chance to break it to some-one new. I'll kick Dervish's ass for spoiling it for me."

"Excuse me," I mutter, exasperated, "but who the hell are you and what are you doing here?"

Bill-E blinks. "No need to speak to me like that," he sniffs. "I'm only trying to be friendly."

"And I just want to know who you are," I respond coolly. "You come in here, telling me your name and that you know all about me, but I've never heard of you before. Are you a relative of Dervish's? A paperboy? What?"

"Paperboy!" he snorts. "I don't think Dervish ever bought a paper in his life! If it doesn't come bound in leather or bat's wings, packed full of spells and dark incantations, he isn't in-terested!"

Bill-E steps to the left, into the light shining through a hole in the roof. "I'm no relative," he says. "Just a friend. I hang out with Dervish, play chess with him, do some odd jobs. He takes me for rides on his bike in return, and teaches me some spells. Has he taught *you* any spells yet?"

I shake my head.

"They're cool." He grins. "I don't know if most of them really work, but the words you use are wicked. I feel like a real magician when I'm casting them."

"Could you teach me some?" I ask.

"No," Bill-E answers promptly. "That's the first thing Dervish taught me — only a teacher is allowed to teach. He says if he ever catches me passing on my spells to anybody, he'll can the lessons and ban me from coming here. And he means it — Dervish isn't the sort to yank your chain about stuff like that."

I'm warming to Bill-E Spleen — I like the way he talks about Dervish — but it's been a while since I made a new friend, so instead of saying something simple, I find myself asking cynically, "Did Dervish tell you to come chat to me? Are you supposed to be my new best friend?"

Bill-E sneers. "My friendship can't be bought or bartered. I usually come over a few evenings every week and on the weekends. Dervish asked me to stay away this week, to give you a chance to settle in. I *was* looking forward to checking you out and showing you around the Vale — as a fellow orphan, I thought we might have stuff in common — but now I don't think I'll bother. You're a bit too up-your-own-ass for my liking. I'll just go see Dervish and leave you to scurry around out here on your own."

Bill-E turns to leave in a huff.

"When did your Mom die?" I ask quietly.

He stops and squints at me. "Nearly seven years ago. I was just a kid."

"And your Dad?"

He smiles crookedly. "I never knew him. Don't even know who he was. He's still alive — I think — so I'm not an official orphan. But I've felt like one since Mom died."

"My folks only died a few months ago," I say. "It still hurts.

A lot. So if I act like a spaz, sorry, but that's just the way I feel right now."

Bill-E's features soften. "When my Mom died, I didn't speak to anyone except Grandma and Grandad for almost a year. If other kids came near, I'd scream and attack them. Their parents stopped them from hitting back. One day, in a shop, I tried it on a kid when there was nobody around — he knocked the crap out of me. I was fine after that."

I offer my chin. "Take a pop if you want."

Bill-E pads over, makes a fist, then taps my chin lightly. "Come on," he laughs. "Let's go see what whirling Dervish is up to."

✠ The study. Dervish and Bill-E catching up. Lots of names I don't recognize. Bill-E talking about school, looking forward to the summer break. Dervish telling him about a new book on Bavarian sorcerors which he bought off the Web.

"What about the eye spell?" Bill-E asks. He looks at me and points to his lazy left eye. "I'm supposed to have this operated on in a few years, but I'm sure Dervish can conjure up a spell to spare me the hassle."

"I've asked around," Dervish laughs, "but the great magicians of yore didn't bother much with drooping eyelids. Besides, magic shouldn't be used for personal gain, Billy." Dervish always refers to Bill-E as Billy. I guess he's known him so long, he finds it hard to change.

"Tell that to great-great-wotsits Garadex!" Bill-E snorts. "He used his magic to make millions, didn't he?"

"Bartholomew Garadex was an exception," Dervish says.

Bill-E treats the study as though it's his own. Pulls books out and only half-pushes them back. Shoves Dervish out of the way to go surfing on the Web. Opens a drawer in the desk to show me the skull of a genuine witch, "burned at the stake for casting lascivious spells on the virile young men of the community," he informs me, waving it around in front of his face, poking his fingers into its empty sockets. Dervish lets Bill-E do as he pleases. Sits back and smiles patiently.

"He's not normally this wound up," Dervish remarks when Bill-E goes to the toilet. "Your arrival upset him. He's used to having the run of the house. I think he's worried that things are going to change now that you've moved in."

"Why does he come here?" I ask.

"His mother and I were friends," Dervish says. "She died in a boating accident, leaving Billy in the care of his grandparents." He pulls a face. "All I'll say about that pair is they're aptly named — *Spleen!* A more cantankerous old couple you couldn't imagine. I felt sorry for Billy, so I started visiting and taking him out on my bike. Ma and Pa Spleen weren't too keen — they still do everything they can to stop his coming over here — but persistence is something I'm good at. I tend to get my own way when I really want to. The odd persuasion spell or two helps." He winks. I can't tell if he's serious or joking.

Bill-E returns, shaking water from his hands. "No towels, Derv," he grumbles.

Dervish raises an eyebrow at me. "Fresh towels are your department, aren't they, Master Grubbs?"

"Sorry." I grimace. "I forgot."

"If I was you, Mr. Grady, sir, I'd sack 'im," Bill-E says with relish, then laughs and asks Dervish to teach him a new spell.

"Will I make the two of you disappear?" Dervish asks innocently.

"Yeah!" Bill-E gasps, face lighting up — then curses as Dervish shoos us out of the room and slams the door shut behind us.

✠ The hall of portraits. Bill-E knows the faces and names off by heart. Giving me a lecture, filling me in on my family background. I listen with pretend politeness, only paying attention to the occasional juicy snippet.

"Urszula Garadex — pirate," Bill-E intones, tapping the frame of a large canvas portrait. The woman in the picture only has one eye, and three of her fingers are missing, two on her left hand, one on her right. "A cutthroat. Utterly merciless.

"Augustine Grady. Servant to some prince or other. Cause of death — he got kicked in the head by a horse.

"Justin Plunkton — a banker. Nothing interesting about him."

And so on.

After a while I ask Bill-E about the teenagers and if he knows how they died.

"Dervish doesn't say much about them," he replies. "I think it's some ancient family curse. *You'll* probably go toes-up any day now."

"I'll try hard to take you with me," I retort.

We come to Dad and Gret. Bill-E pauses curiously. "These are new. I don't know who —"

"My dad and sister," I inform him quietly.

He winces. "I should have guessed. Sorry." He looks at me questioningly, licks his lips, stares back at the photos.

"An unasked question is the most futile thing in the world," I prod him.

"That's one of Dervish's sayings," he notes. Licks his lips again. "Do you want to tell me how they died, or is it a secret? I asked Dervish, but he won't say, and Grandma and Grandad don't know — nobody in the village does."

My stomach tightens. Flashes of a crocodile-headed dog, a hell-child, their eerie master. "They were murdered."

Bill-E's eyes widen. His lazy left eyelid snaps up as though on elastic bands. "No bull?" he gasps.

My expression's dark. "No bull."

"Do you know who did it?"

"I was there."

Bill-E gulps deeply. "When they were being killed?"

"Yes."

"How'd you get away?"

I consider how much I should tell him. Decide to try him with the truth. "They were murdered by demons. I escaped using magic."

He frowns. "If this is a joke . . ." Stops when he sees my face. "Does Dervish know?"

"Yes."

"He believes you?"

"Yes. But he's the only one. Everybody else thinks I'm making it up."

Bill-E grunts dismissively. "If Dervish believes you, so do

I." He turns from the photos and does an odd little shuffling dance, mumbling weird words.

"What was that for?" I ask, bemused.

"One of Dervish's spells," he says. "It makes the dead smile. Dervish says it's important to keep the dead happy. The reason this house isn't haunted is that Dervish keeps its ghosts laughing."

"Bull!" I bellow.

"Maybe," Bill-E grins. "But I've been dancing for years and never been bothered by ghosts. Why stop now and run the risk?"

✚ We watch MTV on the widescreen TV, munching popcorn, drinking Coke from tall paper cups just like in the cinema.

"The TV was my idea," Bill-E brags, the remote control balanced on his left knee. "Dervish resisted to begin with, but I kept on at him and eventually he bought one."

"Does he always cave in to your demands?" I ask.

"No," Bill-E sighs. "I can wrap Grandma and Grandad round my little finger, but Dervish doesn't crumple. He got the TV because I convinced him it was a good idea — his guests would get good use out of it even if he didn't."

"You and Dervish are close, aren't you?" I note.

"Step aside, Sherlock Holmes — there's a new kid in town!" Bill-E chuckles, rolling his eyes.

"I don't want to . . . like . . . get between you . . . or anything," I mumble awkwardly.

"You couldn't if you tried," he responds smugly.

"I could!" I bristle. "He's my uncle."

"So?" Bill-E laughs. "He's *my* father!"

I stare at him, stunned.

Bill-E looks sheepish. "I shouldn't have said that," he mutters. "You won't tell him, will you?"

"No . . . but . . . I mean . . ." I catch my breath. "You said you didn't know your father!"

"I don't," he says. "Not officially. But it hardly takes a genius to work it out. He wouldn't invite me over and make such a fuss of me if we weren't related. And Grandma and Grandad Spleen wouldn't tolerate his involvement unless they had to, no matter how close a friend of Mom's he was. Dervish has to be my dad. It's logic."

"Have you ever asked him?"

Bill-E shakes his head instantly. "Why spoil it? We get along great the way we are. If the truth ever came out, he might decide to sue for custody."

"Wouldn't you like that?" I ask.

He shrugs. "I wouldn't miss Grandma and Grandad that much if I moved in with Dervish," he admits. "I could still go see them all the time. But if he lost, they might take out a court order to stop him seeing me. I reckon they struck a deal with him when Mom died — he could carry on visiting, or having me over to visit, as long as he never told me who he really was. If I go messing about, it might screw up everything."

I scratch my head, thinking that over. It all seems a bit complicated to me — Dervish doesn't strike me as the sort to go in for such subterfuge. But I'm new on the scene. Bill-E has spent most of his life around my uncle. I guess he knows what he's talking about.

"This makes us cousins — if it's true," I note.

"Yeah," Bill-E giggles, then pokes me in the chest. "It also makes *me* his son and rightful heir, so don't go getting too attached to this place, Grady, because as soon as the old man kicks it, you're out of here!"

"Charming!" I laugh, and dump the last of my popcorn over Bill-E's head.

"Hey!" Bill-E shouts, shaking kernels from his head, all over the couch and floor. "Clean that up!"

"*You* clean it," I grin wickedly. "It's *your* house . . ."

Both of us laughing, he chases me up the stairs to my room, lobbing fistfuls of popcorn at my head all the way.

CARNAGE IN THE FOREST

✝ ✝ ✝

ROUTINES. Daily chores. Lots of chess competitions with Dervish and Bill-E. Dervish taught Bill-E how to play. He's much better than I am, though his concentration wanders occasionally, so I beat him more than I should. Watching TV. Hanging out with Bill-E. We play soccer and explore the countryside when we're not stuck in front of the massive screen or locking horns in chess tournaments.

I'm recognized in Carcery Vale now. Bill-E introduced me to the shopkeepers and gossips. They accept me the same as any other kid. Pass the time of day with me when I come in to pick up shopping. Ask about Dervish and what I think of the mansion. Tell me tales from its gory past, trying to spook me.

Bill-E also takes me to visit Grandma and Grandad Spleen. A couple of battleaxes! Narrow-eyed, sharp-tongued, drably dressed, their house in a state of perpetual gloominess. Grandad Spleen rambles on about the old days and how Carcery Vale has gone to the dogs. Grandma Spleen hovers in the background, serving tea and cookies, eyes daring me to spill crumbs on her carpet.

Both have lots to say about Dervish, none of it good.

"Not right, living out there on his own."

"A house like that's too big for one man."

"He should be married — but no one will have him!"

"If he does anything out of order, you let us know."

Bill-E smiles apologetically when we leave. "I love my grandparents, but I know what they're like. I won't take you there too often."

I shrug as if it's no big deal, but offer up silent thanks. I don't know how he stands them. I'd have run away from home years ago if I was caged in with a crabby old pair like that! Although, thinking twice about it, I suppose it's better to have grumpy grandparents as parents than no parents at all. I complained a lot about Mom and Dad when they were . . . still with me. They had their faults. I think everybody does. But I wouldn't complain if they were with me . . . *alive* now.

The murders are never far from my thoughts. The memories of Vein, Artery, and Lord Loss haunt me. Many nights I wake screaming, arms thrashing, eyes wild, imagining demons in the room with me, under the bed, in the wardrobe, scratching at the door.

Dervish is always there when I wake from my nightmares. Sitting by the bottom of my bed. Passing me a mug of hot chocolate or a towel to wipe the sweat from my face. He never says much, or asks what I was dreaming about. Leaves as soon as I've settled down.

We haven't discussed the demons. I think Dervish wants

to, but I'm reluctant to step back into that world of darkness. He leaves books in my room, or open on the tables downstairs, about monsters, demons, magic. I avoid them at first. Later I read certain passages and study pictures, attracted to the mystery of this other realm despite my fears of it.

No pictures of *my* demons in the books. I glance through some of the many encyclopedias in the mansion, but there's no mention of a Lord Loss or his familiars in any of them.

✚ Friday. Listening to CDs I bought in the Vale. A roaring outside, of a motorbike approaching. But it isn't Dervish — he's up in his study. I creep to the window and secretly watch the cyclist dismounting. A woman dressed in black leather. Long blond hair tumbles down over her shoulders when she removes her helmet. She stretches, hands going high above her head. *Ay caramba!*

I'm down the stairs in a flash, but not as fast as Dervish. He's already opening the front doors. I catch a glimpse of a big smile. Then he's shouting, "Meera! I wasn't expecting you for another few days. Why didn't you phone?"

"You never answer," the woman says, meeting Dervish in the doorway, hugging him hard. She pushes him away and studies his face. "How's it going, hon?"

"Not bad," Dervish chuckles.

"How's the house guest?" She spots me over Dervish's shoulder. "Oh, never mind, I'll ask him myself." She strides over and offers her hand. I shake it politely. "Meera Flame," she introduces herself. She smiles — dazzling. "And if I know Dervish, he hasn't told you a thing about me, right?"

I nod dumbly. I think I'm in love!

"Grubbs Grady — Meera Flame," Dervish says. "Meera's a close friend of mine. She comes to stay quite regularly. I meant to tell you she was on her way, but I forgot."

"He's useless, isn't he?" Meera laughs.

"At some things," I mutter, finding my voice at last.

Meera unzips the front of her leather jacket, revealing a T-shirt with an anti-war slogan. She slides out of the coat, then sits on the stairs and peels off her boots and trousers. She's wearing shorts underneath.

"Make yourself at home," Dervish says wryly.

"Don't I always?" Meera replies. She catches me ogling her, and winks. "Got a girlfriend, Grubbs? If not, watch out — I like younger men!"

I blush like a fire engine. Meera slips through to the kitchen for a drink.

Dervish laughs. "You look like a kettle."

I frown. "What do you mean?"

"There's steam coming out your ears!"

Before I can think of a comeback, Meera calls from the kitchen. "Whoops! I've spilled milk all over my T-shirt. Can you come and help me out of it, Grubbs?"

I think life's about to get *very* interesting!

✠ "Ah," says Bill-E with a cheetah's smile. "The mysterious Meera Flame. She's hot, isn't she?"

"And doesn't she know it," I huff. "She hasn't stopped flirting with me since she arrived. My cheeks feel like they've been slapped a dozen times today!"

We're in the kitchen, guzzling milk shakes. Dervish and Meera have gone out for dinner.

"Don't worry about that," Bill-E says. "She does it with me too. She likes making men — and boys! — blush."

"She's doing a good job of it," I mutter, then cough. "Her and Dervish . . . are they . . . ?"

"Nah," Bill-E says. "Just friends. She travels around a lot. Always off somewhere exotic. Comes to stay every now and then. They go on biking trips together sometimes, but Dervish says they aren't an item, and I don't think he'd lie. Who could keep quiet if they had a girlfriend like that!"

✛ Saturday. Meera woke me up this morning for breakfast in bed. Walked right in, wearing a nightgown and (as far as my imagination's concerned) nothing underneath. Sat chatting with me while I ate, asking about life with Dervish and what I thought of Carcery Vale — "Boring as hell, isn't it?" — and just being all-around beautiful. I had a hard time keeping my eyes on my toast and fried eggs!

Bill-E came early to see Meera. She fussed over him like a mother hen. "You've grown! You're filling out! Becoming a man! When are you going to sweep me off my feet and take me away from all this?"

Dervish and Meera made for his study after a while, so Bill-E and I head out to explore the nearby forest. Searching for Lord Sheftree's buried treasure.

"If we find it, we don't tell anyone," Bill-E says, poking through the roots of an old dead oak. "We wait until we're older and know more about these things. Then we sell it on the quiet and split the profits fifty-fifty. Agreed?"

"Maybe I'll bump you off and take it all for myself." I smirk.

"Won't work," he says seriously. "I keep a diary. If I die, Grandma and Grandad Spleen will find it, read about us digging for the treasure, and put two and two together."

"You think of everything, don't you?" I laugh.

"I try to," he says immodestly. "I get it from Dervish and our chess games. He's always nagging me to maximize my potential and use my brain more."

"What is it with him and chess?" I ask. "My mom and dad were the same, like it was the most important thing in the world."

"I don't know about your mom," Bill-E says, "but it's a family tradition on your dad's side. Seven or eight of the clan have been grandmasters. When Dervish talks about his ancestors, he often makes mention of the great chess players. He even judges people by their ability on the board. I asked him about one of his relatives once, a girl who died about thirty years ago — she looked interesting in her photo and I wanted to know what she was like. He just grunted and said she wasn't very good at chess. That's all he had to say about her."

Bill-E decides the treasure isn't buried under the tree. Picking up our tools — an axe and a shovel — we go in search of other likely spots.

"How often do you come searching for this treasure?" I ask.

"It depends on the weather," he answers. "In summer, when it's hot and the evenings are long, I maybe come out three or four times a month. Perhaps only once a month in winter."

"Don't you have any friends?" I inquire bluntly — I've noticed he doesn't talk much about other kids, unless he's chatting about school. And he always has plenty of time for visiting Dervish and me. He never says he can't come or has to dash off early to see another friend.

"Not many," he says honestly. "I have friends in class, but I don't see much of them outside of school. Grandma and Grandad Spleen like to keep me tucked up safe and snug indoors, which is part of the problem. I like hanging out with Dervish, which is another part. I guess mostly I'm just odd, not very good at making friends."

"You made friends with *me* pretty easily," I remind him.

"But you're like me," he says. "An outsider. Different. A freak. We're both weird, which is why we get along."

I'm not sure I like the sound of that — I've never thought of myself as a freak — but it'd be childish to stamp my foot and shout something like, "I'm not weird!" So I let it ride and follow Bill-E deeper into the woods.

✠ In the middle of a thicket. Picking a spot to clear, where we can excavate. I find a patch of soft earth between two stones. I start to dig and earth crumbles away. It looks like there's a hole here. Probably an animal's den, but maybe, just maybe . . .

"I think this might —" I begin.

"Ssshh!" I'm cut short.

Bill-E presses his fingers to his lips — silence. He crouches low. I follow suit. I can tell by his intent expression that this isn't a game. My heart beats faster. I grip my axe tightly. Flashback to *that* room, *that* night. Terror starts to dig its claws in deep.

"I smell him," Bill-E whispers. "If he spots us, laugh and

act as if we were trying to surprise him. If he doesn't, keep down until I tell you."

"Who is it?" I hiss. Bill-E waves the question away and concentrates on the trees beyond the thicket.

Ten seconds pass. Twenty. Thirty. I'm counting inside my head, the way I do when I'm swimming and trying to hold my breath underwater. Thinking — if it's *them*, should I run or try to fight?

Sixty-nine, seventy, seventy-one . . . a pair of feet. Sneakers. Lime green sports socks. I stifle a laugh. It's only Dervish! The terror passes and my heartbeat slows. I make a note to myself to give Bill-E a thumping later for scaring me like that.

Bill-E stays low as Dervish pads past the thicket and moves on through the trees beyond. Then he wriggles out as quietly as possible and gets to his feet, gazing after the departed Dervish.

"What was that about?" I ask, standing, wiping myself down.

"Let's follow him," Bill-E says.

"Why?" I get a thought. "You don't think he's going to meet Meera out here, do you?" I grin slyly and nudge his ribs with an elbow.

Bill-E glares. "Don't be stupid!" he snaps. "Just trust me, OK?" Before I can respond, he slips away in pursuit of Dervish, like an Indian tracker. I lag along a few paces behind, bemused, wondering what this silly game's in aid of and where it's leading.

✠ ✠ ✠

✠ Several minutes later. Hot on Dervish's trail. Bill-E keeps his prey in sight, but is careful not to give himself away. He moves with surprising stealth. I feel like a clumsy bull behind him.

Dervish stops and stoops. Bill-E catches his breath, reaches back, and drags me up beside him. "Can you see?" he whispers.

"I can see his head and shoulders," I grunt in return, squinting. No sign of Meera, worse luck!

"Watch his hands when he rises."

I do as Bill-E commands. Moments later my uncle stands, holding something stiff and red. I get a clearer view of it as he turns to the left — a dead fox, its body ripped apart.

Dervish produces a plastic bag. Drops the fox into it. Studies the ground around him. Moves on.

Bill-E waits a couple of minutes before advancing to the spot where Dervish found the fox. The ground is stained with blood and a few scraps of fur and guts.

"The blood hasn't thickened," Bill-E notes, poking a red pool with a twig, holding it up as though judging the quality of the blood. "The fox must have been killed last night or early this morning."

"So what?" I ask, bewildered. "A dead fox — big deal!"

"I've seen Dervish collect others like that," Bill-E says quietly. "There's an incinerator on the far side of the Vale. Dervish has a key to it. He takes the corpses there and burns them when nobody's around."

"The most hygienic disposal method," I note.

"Dervish doesn't believe in interfering with nature," Bill-E disagrees. "He says corpses are an important part of the food chain, that we should leave dead creatures where we find them — unless they're likely to cause a public nuisance."

"What all this about?" I ask edgily.

Bill-E doesn't answer. He stares at the forest floor, thinking, then turns sharply and beckons. "Follow me," he snaps, breaking into a jog, and I have no option other than to run after him.

✠ A clearing by a stream. Beautiful afternoon sun. I lie down and soak it up while Bill-E drags a large black plastic bag out from under a bush.

"I've collected these over the last three months," he says, untying a knot in the bag's top. "I saw Dervish removing a couple of bodies during the months before that, and thought I'd keep an eye out for corpses and grab hold of them before he did."

He finishes with the knot, clutches the bottom of the bag, and spills the contents out. A swarm of flies rises in the air. The stench is disgusting.

"What the . . . !" I cough, covering my mouth and nose with my hands, eyes watering.

Lots of bones and scraps of flesh at Bill-E's feet. He separates them carefully with a large stick. "A badger," he says, pointing to one of the rotting carcasses. "A hedgehog. A swan. A —"

"What the hell is this crap?" I interrupt angrily. "That stench is enough to knock —"

"I didn't know why I felt I had to hold onto them," Bill-E says softly, eyes on the putrid corpses. He looks up at me. "Now I know — to show them to *you.*"

I stare back uncertainly. This feels very wrong. If Bill-E was trying to gross me out, I could understand — even appreciate — the joke. But there's no laughter in his eyes. No grisly delight in his expression.

"Not you personally," he continues, looking back to the animals. "But part of me must have wanted to show them to somebody. It was just a matter of time until the right person came along."

"Bill-E," I mutter, "you're freaking me out big-time."

"Come closer," he says.

I study his expression. Then the spade lying close to him on the ground. I take a firm grip on my axe. Walk a few steps towards him. Stop short of easy reach.

"Look at them," he says, pointing to the animals.

Like the fox Dervish found, their bodies have been ripped open. Heads and limbs are missing or chewed to pieces. I flash back on images of Dad hanging from the ceiling.

"I'm going to be sick," I moan, turning aside.

"These haven't been killed by animals," Bill-E says. I pause. "Look at the way their stomachs have been ripped apart — jaggedly, but up the middle. And the bite marks don't correspond to any predators I know of. If this was the work of a wolf or bear, the marks would be wider spaced, and larger, because of the size of their jaws."

"There aren't any wolves or bears around here." I frown.

"I know. But I had to assume that it could have been a bear or wolf — or a wild dog — until I was able to examine the corpses in closer detail. I didn't leap to any conclusions."

"But you've come to some since," I note wryly. "So hit me with it. What do you think did this?"

"I'm not sure," Bill-E says evenly. "But I've checked out the teeth marks in the best biology books and Web sites that I could find. As near as I could match them, they seem to belong to an ape —"

"You're not telling me it's King Kong!" I whoop.

"— or a human," Bill-E finishes.

Cold, eerie silence.

✠ Dervish's study. Bill-E leads me in. I'm not sure where Dervish is, but his bike isn't outside, so he's not home. Meera's bike is gone too.

"We shouldn't be here," I whisper anxiously. "Dervish said this room is magically protected."

"I know," Bill-E replies. He steps in front of me, spreads his arms, and chants. I don't know what language he's using, but the words are long and lyrical. He turns as he chants, eyes closed, concentrating.

Bill-E stops and opens his eyes. "Safe," he grunts.

"You're sure?"

"Dervish taught me that spell years ago. He updates it every so often, when he alters the protective spells of the house. It'll probably be one of the first spells he teaches you when he decides you're ready to learn."

I feel uncomfortable, especially since I promised Dervish that I wouldn't come in here without him. But there's no stopping Bill-E, and I'm too curious to back out now.

"What are we looking for?" I ask, following him to one of the bookshelves. He came here directly from the clearing, without saying anything more about the dead animals he'd collected.

"This," Bill-E says, lifting a large, untitled book down from one of the shelves over Dervish's PC. He lays it on the desk but doesn't open it.

"Demons killed your parents and sister," he murmurs. My insides freeze. He looks up. "We inhabit a world of magic. My proposal would make an ordinary person laugh scorn-fully. But we're not ordinary. We're Gradys, descendants of the magician Bartholomew Garadex. Remember that."

He opens the book. Creamy, crinkled pages. Handwrit-ing. I try reading a few paragraphs but the letters are indeci-pherable — squiggles and swirls.

"Is that Latin, Greek, one of those old languages?" I ask.

"It's English," Bill-E says.

"Coded?"

He half-smiles. "Kind of. Dervish cast a reading spell on it. The words are written clearly, but we can't interpret them without unraveling the spell."

Bill-E turns to the first page and runs a finger over the ti-tle at the top. "Lycanthropy through the ages," he intones.

"How do you know that if you can't break the spell?" I challenge him.

"Dervish read it out to me once." He looks at me archly. "Do you know what 'lycanthropy' means?"

"Of course!" I huff. "I've seen werewolf movies!"

Bill-E nods. "Dervish read bits of it to me. They were all to do with werewolf legends and rules. He's fascinated by werewolves — lots of his books focus on shape-changers."

Bill-E flicks to near the end of the book, scans the pages, flicks over a few more. Finds what he's searching for and lays a finger on a photograph. "I discovered this a year or so ago," he says softly. "Didn't think anything of it then. But when I saw Dervish removing the bodies of the animals a few months ago, and found others ripped to pieces . . . always close to a full moon . . ."

"I don't believe where you're going with this," I grumble.

"Remember the demons," he says, and turns the book around so that I can see the face in the photo.

A young man, maybe sixteen or seventeen. Troubled-looking. Thin. His face is distorted — lots of hair, a blunt jaw, sharp teeth, yellow eyes. There's something familiar about the face, but it takes me a few seconds to place it. Then it clicks — it reminds me of one of the faces from the hall of portraits. One that hangs close to Dad and Gret's photos.

"Steven Groarke," Bill-E says. "A cousin. Died seven or eight years ago."

"I met him once," I whisper. "But I was very young. I don't remember much about him. Except he didn't have hair or teeth like that."

Bill-E flicks the pages backwards. Comes to rest on a page with another photo from the hall of portraits, this time a young girl. "Kim Reynolds. Ten years old when she died — supposedly in a fire."

He flicks back further, almost to the start of the book. Stops at a rough hand-drawing of a naked, excessively hairy man, hunched over on all fours like a dog — or a wolf. Razor-sharp teeth. Claws. An elongated head. Yellow, savage eyes.

"That's not a human," I mumble, my mouth dry.

"I think it is — or was," Bill-E contradicts me. "I can't be sure, but I've compared it to a drawing of Abraham

Garadex — one of old Bartholomew's sons — and I'd swear that they're one and the same."

I reach out with trembling fingers and gently close the book. "Say it," I croak. "Say what you brought me here to tell me."

"I'm not saying this to shock you," Bill-E begins. "I wouldn't say it to anyone else. But you were honest enough to tell me about the demons, so I think —"

"Just say it!" I snap.

"OK." Bill-E takes a deep, relaxing breath. "I think those people in the book were shape-changers. I think lycanthropy runs in our family, and has for hundreds, maybe thousands, of years. I think your uncle — my father — has it.

"I think Dervish is a werewolf."

A THEORY

✠   ✠   ✠

"**Y**OU'RE crazy."

Storming down the stairs to the main hall. Bill-E hurrying to catch up.

"It makes sense," he insists, darting ahead of me, blocking my path. "The bite marks. The way the animals were ripped up the middle. Why he collects the carcasses and incinerates them — getting rid of evidence."

"Crazy!" I snort again, and shove past him. "A while ago you told me Dervish was your father — now you think he's a werewolf!"

"What's one got to do with the other?" Bill-E says. "Werewolves are normal people except around the time of a full moon."

"You're barking mad!" I shout, throwing open the front doors, stepping out into welcome sunlight. "This is the twenty-first century. The police have cameras everywhere. DNA testing. All the rest. A werewolf wouldn't last a week in today's world."

"It would if it had human cunning," Bill-E disagrees. "Hear me out, will you? I've been working this through in my head for the last few months. I've got most of it figured."

I stop reluctantly. A large part of me wants to keep on walking and not listen to another word of Bill-E's madness. But a small part is fascinated and wants to hear more.

"Go on," I grunt. "But if you start on about silver bullets or —"

"You think I want to kill him?" Bill-E snaps. "He's my father!"

Bill-E strolls as he outlines his theory. I wander along beside him.

"In movies you become a werewolf if another werewolf bites you. But I don't think dozens of people from one family would get bitten, one after another, over so many centuries. It must be passed on by genes, from parents to children. The unlucky ones are *born* to become werewolves. So I imagine they start to change pretty early, when they're kids or teenagers. Dervish is in his forties. If he is a werewolf, I think he's been living with this for decades.

"Werewolves can't be wild killers," he continues. "If they were, Dervish would have killed loads of people here. I've checked old newspapers in the library — nobody nearby has been killed by a savage beast anytime recently."

"Maybe he roams further afield to do his killing," I insert wryly.

"I thought of that," Bill-E says earnestly. "But I've kept a close eye on him these past few months, and I haven't seen him spending nights away around full moon time. Besides, we've seen some of his local kills — the butchered animals.

If he hunts and kills animals this close to home, there's no reason he shouldn't hunt and kill humans here too. But Dervish isn't a killer. If I thought there was even a slim chance that he was, I wouldn't be talking to you — I'd be telling the police."

"You'd turn in your own father?" I sneer.

"I'd have to if he was killing," Bill-E says softly. "Murderers can't be allowed to roam freely."

We're getting near to the sheds. A large sheet of corrugated iron lies on the ground between the sheds and the mansion. We head for it simply because there's nowhere better to go. This used to be a small orchard. There are several smooth tree stumps closeby. Bill-E sits on one and I sit on another. I tap the corrugated iron with my foot, considering the "evidence."

"So you think Dervish is a werewolf with a conscience. He kills animals but not people."

"Is that so hard to believe?" Bill-E asks. "You accept demons are real — why not werewolves?"

"I accept demons because I've seen them," I answer stiffly. "And I'm sure they're demons twenty-four hours a day, corrupt and evil all the time. If you asked me to believe that people can turn into savage beasts — physically transform into wolf-like creatures — maybe I could. But I don't believe an ordinary human can change into a hairy, yellow-eyed, fanged werewolf overnight, then resume his ordinary shape the next day."

"I never said he transformed," Bill-E notes swiftly. "I think it's more a mental condition than a physical one."

"What about those creatures in the book?"

"Maybe it works different ways in different people," he suggests. "Some get it bad and change completely. Others, like Dervish, are able to control it."

"Degrees of werewolfism," I chortle. "This gets crazier every time you open your mouth."

"OK," Bill-E huffs, getting up, shoulders slumping. "Have it your own way. I thought I was doing you a favor, but if you're going to mock me, I'll just —"

"How do you reckon you were doing me a favor?" I interrupt.

"*I* don't live here," Bill-E says, turning to depart. "Come the next full moon, I'll be tucked up in bed, in the Vale, safe with Gran and Grandad. *You'll* be out here by yourself . . . alone in the house . . . with Dervish."

✠ Hours later. Trying to laugh it off. Craziness. Utter lunacy. I shouldn't even be considering it.

And yet . . .

In a world beset by demons, why shouldn't werewolves exist too? And I can't think why Dervish should be searching the forest for dead animals and burning them secretly. And some of the faces in the book definitely match those in the hall of portraits.

Then again, I only have Bill-E's word that the book is about werewolves. Dervish has a weird sense of humor. He might have been kidding Bill-E about the book. Maybe he even stuck in the photos and drawings himself. That makes more sense than Bill-E's werewolf theories. Much more logical.

And yet . . .

✠ Dervish arrives back just before sunset. I greet him as he enters. "Go anywhere special?"

"Just for a drive," he replies, slicking down his grey hair at the sides of his head.

"Where's Meera?" I ask.

"Off touring the countryside. She's basing herself here for the next week or so, but she'll be coming in and out a lot. Where's Billy?"

"He went home."

"Oh?" Dervish pauses on his way to the bathroom. "I thought he was going to watch TV."

"He had other things to do," I lie.

Dervish continues on to the bathroom. My eyes follow him automatically, studying his face, the set of his jaw, the crown of his head, searching for abnormalities.

✠ Night. Heavy clouds. Only brief glimpses of the three-quarters full moon.

Watching TV with Dervish — a documentary about some Indian woman that he knows. All about using people's natural body energies to cure diseases. Y-A-W-N!

A game of chess afterwards. Dervish appears distracted (or am I imagining it?). Plays loosely, less aggressive than usual. He beats me, but I take a couple of his major pieces and make him work hard for his victory.

Dervish stretches. Groans. Checks his watch. "I'm exhausted. Going to tuck in early. You staying up late tonight?"

I keep my head down. "No. I'm pretty tired too. I'll follow you up soon."

Slyly watching him trot up the stairs — not the pace of a sleepy man heading for bed.

Lining up the chess pieces on the board. Idly playing against myself. Quiet, the house creaking around me, a wind blowing lightly outside.

I abandon the game halfway through. Go up to my room. Pause at the door. This is stupid. If I leave it like this, I'll be imagining danger everywhere I look. I've got to share this house — my life — with Dervish. I can't let something this ridiculous come between us.

Retreating, I carry on up the staircase to the top floor. Dervish's room. I stand outside a moment, getting my story straight, deciding to tell him everything Bill-E said. I grin as I picture his incredulous response. Then I rap twice with my knuckles and enter.

"Sorry to interrupt, but I've got to . . ."

I grind to a halt.

The room is empty.

✠ I've explored the entire house. His study. The bathrooms. The other bedrooms. Downstairs. Even the cellar, in case he's scouring the racks, admiring his wine collection.

He isn't here.

✠ Sitting up in bed. Listening to the wind. Thinking about dead animals and old werewolf films. Afraid to sleep.

✠ ✠ ✠

✢ My eyes snap open. Early morning. Must have dozed off despite my fear. I roll out of bed. Grey day, sky obscured by clouds.

I pad downstairs to the kitchen. Scent of fried bacon and sausages. I push the door open slowly. Dervish inside, at the frying pan, humming. It takes him a moment to spot me. He smiles. "You're up early."

"I didn't sleep very well."

"Hungry?" Dervish asks. "Want some bacon? Eggs?"

"I'll just do toast for myself." I stick two slices of bread in. Pause over the toaster, my back to him. "I went up to see you last night," I say innocently. "Couldn't find you. Were you out?"

The shortest of pauses. Then, "Yeah. I went to a pub in the Vale. Met Meera there. She went on somewhere else afterwards. Sorry I didn't tell you."

"That's OK." I reach for the butter. "Did you take the bike?" If he says he did, I'll know he's lying — I would have heard it.

"No," he says. "I walked. I don't hold with drinking and driving."

I turn from the toaster, smiling. Dervish is concentrating on his bacon. I can't believe I spent so much time worrying last night. I open my mouth to tell him about yesterday's scene with Bill-E.

Then close it.

Dervish is reaching for an egg with his right hand. My eyes are attracted to his nails. Not long — but jagged. Dirty. Red stains under the tips.

It could be paint or rust or something he ate in the pub the night before.

Or it could be *blood*.

Staring. Staring. Staring.

The toaster pops behind me.

I almost scream.

✠ Dragging clothes out of the washing machine. If Dervish walks in on me, I'll say I left money in one of my pockets.

Underpants. Socks. Shirts. Trousers. Finally — a blue denim shirt with a small eagle insignia on the left breast pocket. The shirt Dervish was wearing last night.

I run my nose over it. Unpleasant and sweaty, but not smoky. Not beery. Not like it would smell if he'd spent a few hours in a pub.

✠ Sitting by the phone. I want to call Bill-E, tell him about Dervish disappearing, the blood, the scentless shirt. Except —

He might have gone to the pub like he said.

Maybe he changed shirts before he went out, after I last saw him.

The stains under his nails could have been anything.

If Bill-E hadn't filled my head with garbage, I'd have thought nothing of Dervish slipping out without telling me. It's not the first time he's done it. He gives me plenty of space and freedom, and expects the same in return. Nothing suspicious about that.

But what does he do when he's out by himself? Where does he go? Did he really meet Meera in the Vale? If so, why didn't she come back here with him? And if he changed shirts before he went out, why isn't the one he wore to the pub in the machine with the rest of his dirty laundry?

✠ Carcery Vale. Outside the Lion & Lamb. There are several pubs in the Vale. I want to go into them all to check if Dervish was in town last night.

My story — Dervish lost his watch, and sent me to ask if it had been found. He can't remember which pub he'd been in, so I'm doing the rounds of them all.

Holding me back — somebody might mention my queries to Dervish.

In the end I turn away from the Lion & Lamb and make for home. Not reckless or scared enough to check on Dervish's alibi. Not yet.

✠ Night. Alone in the house. Meera called in this afternoon. I wanted to ask if she'd enjoyed the pub last night, but Dervish was there and I didn't want to be so obvious. They left a few hours ago. Dervish told me they were going into the Vale and not to wait up for them. Asked if I'd like them to bring back anything. I said some chips would be nice.

A truly crazy thought — what if Dervish and Meera are *both* werewolves? I cast that from my thoughts even before it's fully formed.

In one of the spare bedrooms, close to the lower end of the house, where the brick extension is. A clear view of the road from here. The room across the hall has an equally good view of the rear yard and sheds. I've left the window open, so if there are any noises, I should hear them.

Glued to the front window. Hoping to see Dervish and

Meera staggering back from the village, singing drunkenly. Planning cutting comments for Bill-E. Wondering if this is all a big gag designed to scare me. I'll be mad as hell if it is — but relieved at the same time.

✠ After midnight. Eyelids drooping. A clanging noise out back jolts me out of my half-daze.

I bolt through to the back room. Edge up to the open window. Peer out. The clouds aren't as thick as they were earlier. An almost-full moon lights most of the yard, though drifting clouds create random stretched shadows.

Dervish and Meera are by the sheet of corrugated iron where the tree stumps are. They're sliding it over to one side. Behind them, on the ground, half-hidden by shadows, something large wriggles. I train my sights on it. Moments later, the clouds drift on and moonlight falls directly on the creature.

A deer, its four hooves bound together with rope, its snout muzzled.

Dervish and Meera finish with the sheet of corrugated iron. I spot two large wooden doors set in concrete in the middle of the ring of tree stumps. A thick chain and lock. Dervish bends to it, takes a key from his pocket, fiddles with the lock, throws the chain to one side, and hauls the doors open.

Steps leading down beneath the ground. Dervish picks up the deer and drapes it over his shoulders. It struggles. He ignores it and starts down the steps. Meera follows, pausing to swing the doors shut behind her.

Clouds scud across the face of the moon. I stare at the doors in the ground. Silent. White-faced. Petrified.

✠ Waiting for Dervish and Meera to come out. Chewing my fingernails. Going back to my earlier crazy thought — what if they're *both* werewolves? I try to cheer myself up by remembering his oath when I moved in — "You'll be safe here." Wondering if that still holds true.

Minutes pass. Ten. Fifteen. Half an hour.

Thinking — they didn't look different when they took the deer down. No extra hair. No sharp canines. Wearing their normal clothes. They weren't howling at the moon. Dervish was able to insert the key into the lock, so his hands couldn't be twisted into animal-like claws. Not the appearance or actions of werewolves.

Forty-five minutes. Fifty. Coming up to an hour when . . . they reappear.

But not through the doors in the ground — instead, from the kitchen!

They walk out of the house, over to the wooden doors. Dervish takes the length of chain, runs it through the two large handles, then locks it. Both of them carefully slide the sheet of corrugated iron back over the doors, hiding them. They drag their feet over the marks in the dirt left by the corrugated iron, masking the tracks. Wipe their hands clean. Dervish scans the surrounding area one final time, then they return to the house.

As soon as they enter, I close the window and race for my room — I don't want them to find me here.

Under the covers, fully dressed, shaking.

Footsteps on the stairs.

I shut my eyes and feign sleep, expecting Dervish to look in on me. But the footsteps continue up to the top floor — his study.

I wait several minutes. When there are no further sounds, I slip out of bed, undress, and put on my pajamas, then sneak back to the rear bedroom. (I can pretend I'm sleep-walking if they discover me now.)

Studying the sheet of corrugated iron. Picking at the puzzle. Dervish and Meera went down the steps in the rear yard, but came up through the house. There must be a secret passage to somewhere inside the mansion.

Quick calculating. Flash upon the obvious answer — the cellar. The wine just a ruse. Dervish doesn't want to keep me away from the cellar to protect his prize vintages, but to safeguard whatever lies beneath.

✠ Bed. Impossible to sleep. Knees drawn up to my chest. Trembling. Clutching a silver axe that I took from one of the walls. Praying I don't have to use it.

✠ Shortly after dawn. Eyes drooping. Fingers loose on the axe handle.

The door bursts open. Meera barges in. I try to scream but my throat constricts and all I manage is a thin squeak.

Meera's holding a bag. She jabs a hand into it. My imagination fills the bag with all sorts of horrors. I struggle to bring the axe up but it catches on the sheets.

Meera pulls a cluster of objects out of the bag and lobs them at me. I cringe away from her, wishing I could sink through the wall behind me.

Some of the objects strike me dead in the face. I gasp, desperately swat them away, then blink with surprise as I realize what she's throwing —

Chips!

THE CELLAR

✠ ✠ ✠

DERVISH and Meera are still laughing in the morning. "Your face!" Dervish chortles at breakfast. "Like every demon in hell was coming for you!"

As I've noted before, my uncle has a twisted sense of humor.

I say nothing while Dervish and Meera enjoy their little joke, only keep my head down and focus on my food. Dervish doesn't understand why I was so scared. He doesn't know that I saw him with the deer, that I suspect he's a werewolf, that I'm wondering if I can buy silver bullets on eBay. I doubt he'd be laughing if he did.

✠ The house to myself. Dervish's early morning runs usually last forty-five minutes to an hour. Enough time for a quick scouting mission.

I hurry down the stairs to the wine cellar. Pause with my hand on the door. In horror movies, monsters always lurk in the basement. But this isn't a movie. I mustn't succumb to fictional fears — not when I have very real fears to contend with.

Creeping down the steps. Leave the door open. Checking my watch — seven minutes since Dervish left. I'll allow myself half an hour, not a second more.

Pause at the bottom of the steps. Dark and cool. I shuffle forward and an overhead light winks on. Studying the rows of wine' racks. I turn full circle. My heart beats erratically. My legs feel like they belong to an elephant — heavyyyyy. The axe in my left hand looks tiny and ineffective in the glaring light of the cellar.

I stalk the nearest aisle, studying the floor — stone slabs, different shapes, tightly cemented together. I pause occasionally, crouch, and rap a slab with the base of my axe, listening for echoes.

None. Solid.

Left at the end. Exploring a second aisle, then a third, a fourth.

No strange-looking slabs. No echoes anywhere I rap. The joining cement between the slabs unbroken. No trace of a hidden door.

✠ Back where I started. Twenty of the thirty minutes have elapsed. Sweating like a pig who can smell burning charcoal. I'm beginning to think I could be wrong about the cellar. Perhaps the hidden entrance is in one of the ground-floor rooms. But I won't give up yet.

I scout the rim of the room, concentrating on the walls, running my fingers over the rough, dry stone, searching for cracks.

A wine rack — ceiling-high, maybe three meters long — covers one section of the wall. My hopes raise — this could be blocking a secret passage! — but when I lift out a couple of bottles, all I see behind is more stone wall. I remove a few more bottles from various places but nothing out of the ordinary is revealed.

Two minutes left. This is a waste. I'll focus on the rooms above. Perhaps the passageway is hidden behind one of Dervish's many bookcases. I'll start in the main hall and work my way . . .

The thought dies unfinished. As I'm rising to leave, I spot a dark smudge on the floor. Stooping closer, I move my head out of the way of the light and squint for a better view.

It's a semi-circular stain, pale, easily missed. Unmistakably a footprint.

Although there aren't many footprints in the cellar — Dervish keeps it really clean — this isn't the first I've discovered. What sets this one apart from the others is that it faces *away* from the wine rack, and the mark of the heel lies hidden beneath the bottles.

Gotcha!

✠ Watching TV. Nervous. Waiting for Dervish to leave.

There was no time to examine the wine rack. Once I'd noted the print, I came straight up and carefully closed the door behind me. Dervish returned a few minutes later, but I was safe in my room by then, and had splashed my face with cold water to take away the bright red flush I'd worked up in the cellar.

Dervish has spent most of the day since then in his study, as he often does, reading, making phone calls, surfing the Net. Time's dragged for me. I have only one burning desire — to get back down the cellar. Not being able to is driving me crazy.

I've been keeping a close watch on the front door — don't want Dervish slipping out unnoticed. I even leave the bathroom door open when I'm in there, so I'll hear him if he comes down the stairs.

So far, no such luck. But I'm patient. He has to leave eventually. He can't stay cooped up here forever.

✚ Night falls. Dervish still hasn't ventured outside.

Over a late dinner, I ask casually if he has any plans for the night.

"Thought I might hit the pub again," he says, grinning sheepishly.

"Are you meeting Meera?"

"Maybe, maybe not. With the unfathomable Meera Flame, who knows?"

"What's the sudden great attraction about drinking in the Vale?" I ask.

"A pretty new barmaid," he laughs.

"What's her name?"

A pause. Then, quickly, "Lucy."

"Getting anywhere with her?"

"She's slowly warming to my charms," he chuckles. "I'll give it another few nights. If she hasn't bitten by then, I'll cut my losses, maybe take you and Bill-E out to see a movie."

He makes it sound very casual, but I know what he's really doing — giving himself an excuse to stay out after dark for the next few nights, until the full moon has come and passed.

✠ Dervish leaves at 9:48 precisely. He sticks his head in my room as he's going and laughingly tells me not to wait up. I smile weakly in reply and say nothing about the fact that he hasn't changed his clothes, slipped on a nice pair of shoes, combed his hair, or sprayed under his arms with deodorant — all the things he would have done if he'd truly been going out cruising.

My uncle has a lot to learn about the art of espionage!

✠ At the cellar door. Hesitant. I'd rather do this by daylight. Going down this late at night, not knowing how long Dervish will be away or when to expect him back, is far from ideal. I consider waiting until morning, when he goes for his daily jog and I have a guaranteed three-quarters of an hour to play with.

But I've had almost no sleep these last two nights. I'm exhausted. I might snore through my alarm in the morning and wake late, the opportunity missed. I don't dare wait.

Deep breath. Tight grip on my axe. Descent.

✠ The wall on either side of the rack is solid, but when I remove one of the bottles, reach in, and rap on the "bricks" behind, there's a dull echo. Grunting, I grab hold of the edge of the rack and pull.

It doesn't budge.

I exert more pressure — same result. Try the other side — no go.

Stepping back. Analyzing the problem. Look closer at the wooden rack. There's a thin divide down the middle. I grab sections of the rack on either side of the divide and try prying them apart. They give slightly — a fraction of an inch — then hold firm.

Brute force isn't the answer. I'm convinced the divide is the key. I just have to figure out how to use it.

Studying the rack. My fingers creep to the top of one of the bottles. Idly twirl it left and right while my brain's ticking over.

I'm taking a step to the left, to check the sides of the rack again, when I stop and gaze down at my fingers. I half-pull the bottle out, then push it back in. Smiling, I grab, twist and pull the bottle above, then the one beside it. All are loose, but I'm sure, if I go through every bottle on the rack, I'll find one that isn't.

Methodical. Start from the bottom left, even though I suspect the device will be situated higher, towards the middle. Checking each bottle in turn, twisting it, tugging it out, placing it back in its original position. I'm leaving fingerprints all over the place — should have worn gloves — but I'll worry about that later.

All the way across to the right. Up a row. Then all the way across to the left. Up and across. Up and across. Up and . . .

✠ Getting higher. Minutes ticking away. I quicken my pace, anxious to make progress. Pull too hard on one bottle. It comes flying out and drops to the floor. I collapse after it and catch it just before it hits and smashes into a hundred pieces. Place it back on the rack with shaking fingers. Work at a steady, cautious pace after that.

✠ Past the midway mark. Four rows from the top, on the right. My hopes fading. Trying to think of some other way to part the racks. Half-tempted to take my axe to the wood and chop through. I know that's crazy, but I'm so wound up, I might just —

Seventh bottle from the right. I twist but it doesn't move. Everything stops. My breath catches. Step up close to the bottle and examine it. No different from any of the others, except it's jammed tight into place. I give it a harder shake, to make sure it isn't simply stuck. No movement at all.

I try pulling the bottle out — it doesn't give.

Studying it again, frowning. My eyes focus on the cork. I grin. Put the tip of my right index finger to the face of the cork. Push gently.

The cork sinks into the bottle. A loud click. The two halves of the wine rack slide apart, revealing a dark corridor angling gently downwards. I do a quick mental geographical check — it leads in the direction of the sheds.

I act before fear has a chance to deter me. Step forward. Cross the threshold. Advance.

✠ I've taken no more than eight or nine steps when the wine rack closes behind me with a soft slishing sound. I'm plunged into total darkness. My heart leaps. My hands strike out to touch the walls on either side, just so I have the feel of something real. Split-seconds away from complete panic when . . .

. . . lights flicker on overhead. Weak, dull lights, but enough to illuminate the tight, cramped corridor.

My heart settles. My eyes devour the light. I smile feebly at myself. Turn and retrace my steps. Examining the back of the wine rack, thinking about how I'm going to get out later. A button in the wall to my left. I press it. The lights flick off and the rack slides open.

I step through to the wine cellar, wait for the rack to close, then open it again and return to the corridor. This time I keep on walking when the rack closes and I'm plunged into temporary darkness. Moments later, when the lights flicker on, I glance up at them wryly and give them a carefree half-wave.

Grubbs Grady — Mr. Cool!

✠ The corridor runs straight and evens out after twenty yards or so. Narrow but high. Moss grows along the walls and ceiling. The floor's lined with a thin layer of gravel. By the moss, I figure this tunnel must be decades old, if not centuries.

The tunnel ends at a thick, dark wooden door, with a large gold ring for a handle. I press my ear to the door but can hear nothing through it. If Dervish is in the room beyond, it'll be impossible to surprise him. I'll just have to cross my fingers and hope for the best.

I take hold of the huge gold ring. Tug firmly. The door creaks open. I enter.

✠ A large room, at least the size of the wine cellar. Sturdy wooden beams support the ceiling. Burning torches set in the walls — no electrical lights. A foul stench.

I leave the door open as I step into the room and study my

surroundings. A steel cage dominates the room, set close to the wall on my right. Almost the height of the ceiling, thin bars set close together, bolted to the floor in all four corners.

Inside the cage — the deer. Still bound and struggling weakly. Lying in a pool of its own waste. Which explains the smell.

Advancing, giving the cage a wide berth. There are three small tables in this subterranean room. Legs carved to resemble human forms. Surfaces overflowing with books. A chess set half hangs off of one of them. Pens. Writing pads. Candles waiting to be lit.

Ropes and chains in one corner. No weapons. I thought there'd be axes and swords, like inside the house, but there isn't even a stick.

A chest — *treasure!* I snap it open in a rush, treasure-lust momentarily getting the better of my other senses. Is this Lord Sheftree's legendary hoard?

Bitter disappointment — the chest's filled with old books and rolled-up parchment. I scrape the paper aside and explore the bottom of the chest, in search of even a single gold nugget or coin, but come up empty-handed.

Circling the room. Get close to the cage this time. Note a bowl set in the floor — for water, I assume. A door with two locks, neither currently bolted. No hatch for pushing food through.

I consider dragging out the deer and setting it free, but that would reveal my having been here. I don't want Dervish knowing I'm wise to this setup. Not sure what he'd do to me if he found out.

Examining the tables. On two of them the books are layered with dust, the candles have never been used, and the chairs are shoved in tight. On the other there are fewer books — a couple are open; the two large candles on the table are both half burned down, and the chair's been pulled out.

I focus on the third table. Walk around it twice without touching it. Wary of magic spells and what might happen if I disturb anything.

I wish Bill-E was here. I should have phoned him and cooked up some story to get him to stay the night. But I didn't want to drag him into this until I was sure — which I'm still not. So far I've seen nothing to suggest that Dervish is a werewolf, or that he uses this cell for anything more sinister than holding captured deer.

I have to take a chance with the spells. I pull the chair back a bit more, then sit and cautiously lay my hands on top of the table.

Nothing happens.

The light's poor here. There are matches on the table but I daren't light a candle — Dervish might smell it when he returns, or notice that it's burned down more than when he left.

I study one of the open books but I can't make sense of the words. If it's in English, it's protected by reading spells, like the books in Dervish's study.

I flick forward a few pages, keeping a finger on the page it was originally opened to. No pictures, though there are a few mathematical or magical diagrams. I turn the pages back and pick up one of the other books.

A wolf's bared jaws flash at me! I gasp — raise my hands to protect myself — almost topple out of my chair —

Then laugh hysterically as I realize it's just the cover of a book under the one I picked up. I need to get a grip. Freaking out over a picture — seriously uncool!

Laying the upper book aside, I open the one with the picture of a wolf on it. The words in this are also undecipherable, but there are many pictures and drawings — most of creatures which are half-human, half-wolf.

I study the photos and illustrations in troubled silence. The paintings are wilder — men with perfectly normal upper halves, but the lower body of a wolf; women with ordinary bodies and twisted wolfen heads; babies covered in hair, with ripped lips and jagged fangs. But the photos are more disturbing, even though they're less grisly than the paintings. Most simply depict malformed humans, with lots of hair, distorted faces, sharp teeth, and slit eyes.

The reason they're so unsettling — they're *real*.

The paintings could be the work of an artist's vivid imagination, but the photos are genuine. Of course I'm aware that it's a simple matter in this day and age to forge photographs and warp reality, but I don't think these are the result of some lab developer's sick sense of humor. This book has the look and feel of an ancient tome — though some of the snaps are in color, the colors are dull and splotchy, like in very old photos. I don't think the people who put this together had the technical know-how to produce digitally enhanced images.

The creatures in the book don't look familiar, though I

study their faces at length. If there are Gradys or Garadexes in there, I don't recognize them.

Closing the book, I pick up another lying to the right. This one's modern. Glossy photos, mostly of dead human-wolf beasts, showing them cut open, their insides scooped out. I can't read it, but I know what it is — an autopsy manual. Somebody's undertaken a study of these wolfen humans and published their findings.

I grin shakily as I imagine what would happen if I went into a library and asked if they had any books on werewolf autopsies!

As I lay the autopsy book aside, my eyes fall on a thin volume. Loose sheets, held together by a wrinkled brown leather folder. Opening it, I find myself staring into the red eyes of the demon master — Lord Loss.

My fingers freeze. My throat pinches shut. It's not the picture Dervish showed me when he came to visit me in the institute. This one's more detailed. It shows only the demon's head. With terrified fascination I study the folds of lumpy red skin, its bald crown, small mouth, sharp grey teeth. Its eyes are especially strange — as I noted before, it seems to have only a dark red iris and pupil.

Trembling, I start to turn the drawing over, to check on the other papers in the folder —

— then stop dead at a terrible whisper.

"Hello . . . Grubitsssssssssssch . . ."

The demon's voice! I release the paper and stare at the painted face — which, impossibly, nightmarishly — *stares back.*

"Release me," the demon on the page whispers, its thin lips moving ever so slightly, its eyes narrowing fractionally. "I hunger for . . . your pain."

The painting grins.

I scream, slam the folder shut, and race, sobbing, for safety, imagining the demon master breathing down my neck every frantic step of the way.

THE LONGEST DAY

✠   ✠   ✠

M Y bed. Curled into a ball on top of it. Weeping. Shaking. Fingers over my eyes. Peeping through them at fitful intervals, waiting for the demon master and his cohorts to come.

✠ Hours later. Footsteps on the stairs. My heart almost stops.

Panting. Eyes wide. Remembering the carnage — Mom, Dad, Gret. Praying it's quick. I don't want to suffer. Maybe I should take the blade of the axe to my throat before the demons . . .

Whistling — *Dervish!*

I moan with relief. The footsteps stop, then start towards my room. I scurry underneath the covers and draw them up around my chin.

Dervish opens the door and sticks his head in. "You OK, Grubbs?" he asks.

"Yes," I answer weakly. "Just a bad dream."

"I can sit with you if you want."

"No. I'm fine. Really."

"See you in the morning then."

"'Night."

He only half-closes the door when he leaves. I want to rush to it and slam it all the way shut, but I don't dare step off the bed — afraid Vein or Artery might be lying beneath, waiting to snap at my ankles and drag me off into their world.

✠ Dawn takes an age to come, but eventually the sun rises and burns my fears away with its cleansing rays.

As the sun clears the horizon and chases the shadows of night westward, I crawl out of bed, over to the window, and throw it open. The morning air is chilly but welcome. I gulp it down like water, my head clearing, my shakes subsiding.

Did the painting really talk to me or did I just imagine it?

I honestly don't know. I *think* it was real. But I was extra tense. Overreacting to everything. It could have been a hallucination.

What was definitely real — the werewolf photos. I didn't imagine *them.* They're what I must focus on. The Lord Loss mystery can wait. I went down the cellar to find evidence of a werewolf. And I believe I found it.

Time to call in the expert.

"Paging Bill-E Spleen . . ."

✠ I phone while Dervish sleeps. Ma Spleen answers, even grumpier than usual. "It's seven twenty-three!" she snaps. "He's still asleep and so was I!"

"Please," I say calmly. "This is important. I want to catch him before he goes to school."

"If you tell me, I can give him a message," she sniffs.

"No," I insist. "I have to speak to him in person."

She grumbles some more, but eventually goes to wake the snoozing master Spleen.

"This had better be life-or-death," Bill-E yawns down the line a minute later.

"You've got to come over," I tell him directly. "Pretend you're going to school, then come here."

"What?" he grunts. "Have you lost your mind? I can't fart in these parts without Grandma knowing. Skipping school is out of —"

"There's a full moon tonight," I hiss. "I don't want to be trapped here alone with Dervish."

A cautious pause. "What's happened?" Bill-E asks.

"Come over. Find out."

I put the phone down before he can ask any further questions, confident that his curiosity will entice him. Start thinking about what I'm going to tell Dervish to explain Bill-E's being here.

✠ He arrives at 9:17, schoolbag slung across his back, left eye squinting suspiciously, black hair slick with sweat — he must have run.

"Couldn't come any earlier or Grandma would have been suspicious," he says, entering by the huge front doors, which I hold open for him like a butler. He looks around like a detective. "Where's Dervish?"

"In his study. I told him you were coming to work on a school project with me."

"He believed that?" Bill-E snorts.

"He had no reason not to. He doesn't know we know about him."

Bill-E looks at me smugly. "So you think I'm telling the truth now?"

I lead him through to the kitchen before answering. "Yes."

"Coolio! What changed your mind?"

I sit down. So does Bill-E. "I've seen his lair," I mutter, and proceed to tell him everything about the deer and my exploration of the wine cellar and the sub-cellar beyond (only leaving out the section relating to Lord Loss — that's personal).

✠ Ten-fifteen. Bill-E arguing that Dervish doesn't pose a threat.

"Don't you see?" he groans with exasperation. "The cage is for *him!* He knows the change is upon him. That's why he caught the deer and stuck it in there. Tonight he'll lock himself in, and when he changes he'll feed on the deer and stay caged there until morning."

"How will he get out?" I ask.

"Meera. That must be why she's here. She knows about his sickness and probably comes every month to help him."

"Think back," I urge him. "You say you've been watching Dervish every time there's been a full moon. Has Meera been here? Or anybody else?"

Bill-E shifts uncomfortably. "Well, not *every* time. But —"

"So how does he get out?" I interrupt.

Bill-E thinks a moment. "He must hang the key nearby," he says. "He lets himself out when the change has passed."

"Then what's to stop him using it when he transforms?"

Bill-E rolls his eyes. "Have you ever heard of a wolf that can use a key?"

"He used it the other night. When he brought the deer back."

"But he hadn't transformed then," Bill-E notes. "You said he looked the same as always." He stands and paces around the kitchen as he outlines his thoughts.

"This is the way it must work. During the lead-up to the full moon — and for a few nights after — Dervish's hormones are all over the place. I don't think he physically changes, but he isn't in full control of himself, which is why he wanders around the forest, hunting animals. At the same time, he's human enough not to attack people. He doesn't kill.

"On the night of the full moon, it's different. The beast comes to the fore. It takes over. He can't risk loosing it on the world. It would kill at random — animals, humans . . . whatever it found.

"So he chains himself up." Bill-E clicks his fingers with excitement. "He locks himself in the cage, ensuring there's a live animal for the beast to rip to pieces and feed on. He stays there all night, howling, transformed, wild. In the morning, when the phase passes, he lets himself out and carries on as normal."

Bill-E stops and smiles warmly. "I've always admired Dervish, but never as much as I do right now. He's dealing with his curse. Living as normal a life as he can, yet protecting the world from the monster within him, locking himself away when he must, enduring the loneliness and hardship . . ."

"Stop," I remark sarcastically. "You'll make me cry."

Bill-E whirls on me angrily. "What did you call me for?" he barks. "If it was just to sneer, I can leave as quickly as I came!"

"It wasn't to sneer," I mumble. "I asked you here to help." I stare miserably at him. "I'm scared. If he changes tonight and comes after me . . ."

"He won't," Bill-E says confidently. "The cage is there to prevent that."

"Maybe." I nod. "But I'm not sure I want to run the risk. I was thinking I could maybe come stay with you for a night or two . . . ?"

Bill-E blinks. "I've never had a friend over to stay," he says. "I don't think Grandma and Grandad would like it. Especially not after you woke them up this morning." His face brightens. "Tell you what. I have a better idea — I'll come and stay here!"

"What will that achieve?" I frown.

"I'm fatter than you," he laughs, patting his stomach. "If the werewolf gets free, it'll go for me first, since I'm so tasty-looking. That'll give you a chance to run for freedom."

"You're crazy," I huff.

"Of course I am," he smiles. "After all, I'm a Grady!"

✠ A long, tense day. Bill-E, despite his good-humored assertions that we have nothing to be afraid of, is just as nervous as me. In some ways he's worse — he looks very pale, and has been sick a couple of times. He says it's some bug he's had for the last few days, but I'm sure it's nerves.

"Maybe you should go home," I suggest as he returns from his latest vomit trip to the toilet. "You won't be much use throwing up all the time."

"Don't be too sure," he smiles thinly. "Perhaps I can repel the werewolf with puke."

"That's one I never saw in the movies!" I laugh.

Bill-E has to leave in the afternoon, to check in with Ma and Pa Spleen and pretend he's been to school. "I'll have a quick meal, do some homework, then tell Grandma I'm coming here for the night — I'll say it's part of a nature project, that I'm doing an essay on the habits of nocturnal creatures."

"Not so far from the truth," I grimace.

✛ In my room. Alone. A knock on the door — Dervish. "Where's Bill-E?"

"He had to go home."

"That's a shame — I was going to cook pancakes. I have a sudden craving for them."

I start to tell Dervish that Bill-E's returning to stay the night. Before I can, he says, "I have to head out later."

"Oh?"

"I'm meeting Meera. We're going to see some old friends. I could be gone all night. You'll be OK by yourself?"

I nod wordlessly.

"I'll give you a shout before I go," he promises.

✛ On the phone to Ma Spleen, asking for Bill-E. "He just got home from school," she says frostily. "He's eating."

"It's important."

"Everything seems to be important today," she grumbles, but calls him to the phone.

"When you return, enter by the back door and try not to let Dervish see you," I tell him.

"Why?" he asks.

"He just told me he's going out for the night. He thinks I'm going to be here by myself."

"So?"

"Let's quit with the seen-it-all, done-it-all act," I snap. "If Dervish is what we think, there could be trouble tonight — *real* trouble. If he doesn't know you're in the house, he won't expect to find you if he gets free later. That might work in our favor in case of an attack."

"There won't be an attack," Bill-E insists.

"Maybe — but come in by the back anyway, OK?"

A moment's pause. Then, in a subdued tone, Bill-E mutters, "OK."

✠ Bill-E sneaks in without Dervish spotting him. Hides in my room. We keep the door shut and our voices low when we speak — which isn't often. I keep a firm hold on the axe I've been lugging about for the past few nights. Bill-E still doesn't believe we're in any danger, but he has a short sword lying on the bed close by, which I fetched for him from downstairs.

He's in a terrible state, white and shivering. He's been sick three times in the space of the last couple of hours. I see now that it isn't nerves — he really is ill.

"You should be home in bed," I whisper as he wraps blankets around himself and gulps down a glass of warm milk.

"I feel like death," he groans, eyes watering.

"Do you want to leave?"

He shakes his head firmly. "Not until morning. I'm going to see this through with you, to prove that Dervish isn't a killer."

"But what if —"

He stops me with a quick cutting motion. "He's coming!" he hisses, and tumbles off the bed, dragging his blankets and empty glass with him, lying flat on the floor, holding his breath.

I sit up in bed and open a comic, which I pretend to read.

Moments later, Dervish knocks and enters. "Coming for dinner?"

"No thanks — not very hungry tonight."

He sniffs the air, nose crinkling. "It smells of sick in here."

"Yeah." I laugh sheepishly. "I threw up earlier. Think it was something I ate."

"You should have told me." He walks over and lays the back of his hand against my forehead. If he bends forward just an inch more, he'll spot the prone Bill-E Spleen . . .

"No fever," Dervish says, stepping back.

"Of course not. Like I said — something I ate."

"I hope that's all it is." He looks troubled. Checks his watch, then glances out the window. "If you get sick again later, I won't be here to drive you to the doctor. Maybe I should take you into the Vale for the night."

"That's OK," I say quickly. "I'm fine."

"You're sure?"

I cross my heart and smile blithely. "Never felt better."

"Hmm . . ." He doesn't look happy, but takes me at my word. "Want me to bring you up anything from the kitchen?"

"No, thanks — I'll wander down later and grab something light."

"See you tomorrow then."

"Tomorrow." I smile, and hold the smile in place until he exits.

"Phew!" I gasp when the coast is clear. "You can get up now."

Bill-E rises from behind the bed like a ghost, grinning sickly. Then his face blanches, and he clutches his stomach and rushes for the toilet.

I raise my eyes to the heavens and sigh. Of all the nights he could have picked to be sick, why this one!

✠ Night. The moon rising. A roar from the corridor — "I'm off!"

"'Bye!" I shout in reply. A quick shared glance with Bill-E, then we both rush to the room behind this one — with a view of the rear yard — and press up against the circle of stained glass, watching to see what Dervish does.

"Bet he heads straight down the cellar," Bill-E says confidently.

"I hope so," I sigh.

Moments later Dervish emerges and walks to the sheet of corrugated iron close to the sheds. He carefully removes it, unlocks the chains, and casts them aside. Bill-E's smiling knowingly — but the smile fades when Dervish drags the sheet of corrugated iron back over the doors, turns, and heads off in the direction of the forest.

"What do we do now?" I ask quietly.

"He might just be going to . . ." Bill-E starts, but hasn't the heart to finish.

"Two choices," I growl. "We let him go — or we follow."

"You want to go into the forest after him?" Bill-E asks uncertainly. "If he transforms out there and the beast spots us . . ."

"At least we know what to expect, and we're prepared," I grunt, hefting my axe. "Nobody else knows what he is. If we let him go and he kills . . ."

Bill-E rolls his eyes, but says sullenly, "We'll follow."

Hurrying from the room. In the hall downstairs, Bill-E stops to grab a sword, longer and sharper than the one I gave him earlier. While he's at it, he plucks a couple of knives, sticks one in his belt, hands the other to me. "Double security," he says.

"I like your thinking." I grin shakily.

Then we're gone — frightened, courageous, crazy — tracking a werewolf.

AROOOOO!

✛   ✛   ✛

SLIPPING away from the house. Creeping around the sheds. Entering the forest. Moving cautiously, Bill-E leading the way. A bright night. Very few clouds to block out the worryingly full moon. But dark under cover of the trees. Countless spots where a creature could lie in ambush.

"Which way did he go?" I whisper as Bill-E pauses and stoops.

"That way," Bill-E replies a few seconds later, pointing left.

"How do you know?"

"Footprints," he says, tapping the ground.

"Who made you Hia-bloody-watha?" I scrunch up my eyes but can't see any prints. "Are you sure?" I ask, wondering if he's deliberately leading me astray.

"Positive," Bill-E says, then stands and stares at me, troubled. "If he sticks to this course, he's heading for the Vale."

I stare back silently. Then we both turn without a word and resume the chase — faster, with more urgency.

✠ ✠ ✠

✠ Running. Ducking low-hanging branches. Leaping bushes.

Bill-E comes to a sudden halt. I run into him. Stifle a cry.

"I see him," Bill-E says softly. "He's stopped."

I peer ahead into the darkness — can't see anything. "Where?"

"Over there." Bill-E points, then crouches. I squat beside him. "We're on the edge of the forest. Carcery Vale's only a minute's jog from here."

"You think he's going to attack someone in the village?" I ask.

Bill-E tilts his head uncertainly. "I can't believe it. But I don't see any other reason why he would come here. Maybe —"

He spins away abruptly, covering his mouth with his hands. Lurches through the bushes. Twigs snap. Leaves rustle. He collapses to the ground and throws up over a pile of twigs.

My gaze snaps from Bill-E to the trees ahead. Clutching the handle of my axe so tightly it hurts. Waiting for Dervish to hear the commotion and come investigate.

Half a minute passes. A minute. No movement ahead.

Bill-E shuffles up beside me. Rests in the shadow of a thick bush. Breathing heavily. Chin specked with vomit. "I can't go on," he groans. His voice cracks as he speaks. His whole body's trembling.

"How bad are you really?" I ask, searching for him in the shadows, only able to make out the dark outline of his face.

"Lousy." He chuckles drily. "I should have listened to you earlier — gone home to bed. I need a doctor."

"Your house isn't far from here," I note. "I could take you there."

"What about Dervish?"

"Is he still where you said he was?" I ask.

Bill-E parts the bush above him, half-kneels, and stares dead ahead. Silence for a few seconds. Then — "Still there."

"I'll take you home," I decide, "then circle back."

"But you can't track him like I can," Bill-E demurs. "You need me."

"I'll get by," I override him. "The way you are now, you're a liability. It's only pure luck that he didn't hear you a few minutes ago. You're useless like this."

"Grubbs Grady," Bill-E giggles hoarsely. "Tells it like it is."

"Come on," I mutter, offering him a hand up. "The quicker we go, the sooner I can pick him up again."

Bill-E hesitates, then grabs my sleeve and staggers to his feet. "Sorry about this," he mumbles, bent over, hiding his face, ashamed.

"Don't be stupid," I smile, wrapping an arm around him. "I couldn't have tracked him this far without you. Now — let's go."

✠ Bill-E's house lies almost straight ahead, but Dervish is blocking the direct route. So we skirt around him and stumble farther through the forest, until we find a spot downhill where he hopefully won't be able to see us.

"Walk or run?" I ask.

Bill-E doesn't answer immediately — his breath is ragged and he's trembling. Then he sighs and says, "Walk. More noise . . . if we run."

Holding Bill-E tight — I think he'd collapse if I let go — I start ahead, into the moonlit clearing.

Stomach like a coiled spring as we leave the cover of the forest. I face forward, not wanting to trip over anything, but my eyes keep sneaking left, scouring the trees for signs of my uncle.

"Can you see him?" I hiss out of the side of my mouth.

Bill-E only groans in reply and doesn't look round.

Getting close to the houses on the outskirts of Carcery Vale. Dark backyards. Lights in kitchen and bedroom windows. A woman cycles towards us, parallel to the forest. She waves. I start to wave back. Then she turns right and I realize she was only signaling.

Coming up to the houses. There's a road behind them, where most of the residents park. We take the road and close in on the Spleen residence. I start to think about what Ma Spleen is going to say, and what will happen when she phones Dervish to complain about the condition he let her grandson walk home in. Perhaps I should take Bill-E directly to a doctor. It's late, but I'm sure —

Bill-E gasps painfully and collapses. He dry retches and paws at the pavement, whining like a wounded animal.

"What's wrong?" I cry, dropping beside him. I reach to examine his face, but he brushes my hands away and snarls.

"Bill-E? What is it? Do you want me to —"

"Grubbs — step away."

A harsh voice, straight ahead of me. Slowly, trembling, I stand and stare.

Dervish!

✚ My uncle's standing between us and the rear garden gate of Bill-E's home. No way past. He's illuminated by moonlight. A long hypodermic syringe in his right hand. Eyes ablaze with anger. "Meera," he says, gaze flicking to a spot behind me. I glance back. A moment's pause, then Meera steps out from behind a van. My head spins. I remember an earlier mad thought — What if they're *both* werewolves?

Dervish starts walking towards me.

"Stop!" I moan, warning him off with my axe.

"Step away, Grubbs," he says again, not slowing. "You don't know what's happening." Then, to Meera, "Be careful. Block his escape, but don't get too close."

"I know what you are," I sob, tears of fear springing to my eyes. "If you come any closer . . ."

"Don't interfere," Dervish snaps. "I don't want to hurt you, but if you don't step aside, I'll —"

He comes within range. I swing at him with my axe. Tears impair my aim — I swing high. Dervish curses and ducks. I take another blind swing. He shimmies closer as I'm swinging, dodges the blade, chops at my axe arm with his free left hand.

My arm goes numb from the elbow down. The axe drops to the ground. I dart after it. Dervish grabs the back of my collar and yanks me aside. I crash into a car. He's upon me before I have time to recover. Wraps his left arm around my throat. Exerts pressure.

"Dervish!" Meera gasps.

"It's OK," he pants. Then, to me, as I struggle for my life, "Easy! We're on the same side."

"Let go!" I wheeze. "I know what you are! Let —"

Low growling. Animalistic. Wolfen.

But not from Dervish.

From ahead of us.

Dervish releases me. I stand rooted to the spot. Eyes wide. Staring at the beast as it rises to its feet and snarls. A contorted face. Yellow eyes. Sharp cheekbones. Dark shadows. Open mouth full of bared teeth.

It raises a hand — dark skin, long nails, fingers curled into claws.

And I realize, about a million years late, that a monster *has* breached the barriers of Carcery Vale tonight — but it's not Dervish.

The werewolf's Bill-E Spleen!

FAMILY TIES

✠   ✠   ✠

"BILL-E?" I moan. He glares at me, naked hate filling his
abnormal yellow eyes. "Bill-E . . . it's me . . . Grubbs."

"He doesn't recognize you," Dervish says, stepping to the
left. Bill-E's eyes snap to the adult and he crouches defensively. Behind him, Meera takes an automatic step backwards. "No!" Dervish barks. "Don't move! You'll attract —"

Too late. Bill-E's head swivels. He spots Meera. Leaps.

Meera gets out the start of a scream. Then the beast is upon
her, hissing as he hauls her to the ground. They land hard,
Meera underneath. She tries to throw the animal off. He grabs
her hand and bites hard into the flesh. She starts to curse, but
is cut short by the creature's fist — it crushes into the side of
her face. Meera chokes, stunned. The beast grabs both sides of
her head and smashes her skull down hard on the pavement.
The fight goes out of her. Teeth glinting in the moonlight, fas-
tening around Meera's throat. The monster's about to rip her
head off and all I can do is stand here and gawk like an idiot.

But Dervish isn't so helpless. He moves as fast as Bill-E, and gets there a split-second before he bites. Grabbing Bill-E's ear, he tugs hard. The creature's head jerks clear of Meera's throat. He whines and lashes out. Dervish ducks the blow. Shoves the animal down hard, headfirst. Pins it with his right knee, digging it hard into the boy-beast's back. Brings up his right hand and jabs the tip of the syringe into the side of Bill-E's neck. Pushes on the plunger. The liquid in the barrel disappears into Bill-E's veins.

Bill-E stiffens and groans. Dervish whips the syringe out and tosses it aside. Bill-E thrashes wildly. Dervish uses both hands and knees to hold him down.

Mad seconds pass. Bill-E stiffens again. More thrashing. Stiffens for the third time — then collapses, eyes closing, limbs limp.

Dervish lays Bill-E's head down, then shoots to Meera's side. "Meera?" he mutters, checking her pulse, putting his ear to her lips, rolling her eyelids up. No response. He straightens her legs and arms, checks on Bill-E, looks around to see if anybody's noticed the scuffle — but the road is deserted except for us. He then turns to face me.

"You bloody fool," he snarls.

I stare blankly at my uncle, then slide to the ground and give myself over to bewildered tears.

✠ Dervish lets me cry myself dry, then hands me a handkerchief and says gruffly, "Clean yourself up, then help me with Billy and Meera."

I wipe my face with the handkerchief. Stand, still sniffling.

"You thought *I* was a werewolf?" Dervish asks.

"Yes," I answer hollowly.

"You ass," he says, and manages a ghost of a smile. "There's nothing more dangerous than someone half-close to a terrible truth. What would you have done if I was? Taken that axe to me? Chopped me up into little bits? Buried me in the forest and told the police I'd gone out walking and never returned?"

"I don't know," I moan. "We didn't think that far ahead. We thought you'd lock yourself up in the cage in the cellar. When you started for the Vale, we —"

"You know about the cellar?" he interrupts. "You've been there?"

"Yes. Not Bill-E — just me. I saw the cage, the deer, the books . . ."

Dervish snorts, disgusted. "I knew you'd sniff it out eventually, but not this quick. I underestimated you — *Sherlock* Grady."

He bends and ties Bill-E's legs together, then his hands. He slips a gag between the unconscious boy's jaws, then picks Bill-E up and drapes him over his shoulders, much as he carried the captured deer.

"What are you going to do with him?" I whimper, flashing on images of Dervish cutting Bill-E's throat, or caging him up for life.

Dervish grunts. "We'll discuss that later. First we have to get him home. He'll be safe once we lock him in the cage — there's water, and he can feed on the deer. We're exposed here."

"But —" I begin.

"Save it," Dervish snaps. "We need to move — *now!* I don't want to be the one to try explaining to Ma Spleen that her grandson's a werewolf!"

I smile fleetingly, then put the questions on hold. Dervish carries Bill-E to the van that Meera had been hiding behind. He pulls the rear door open and bundles Bill-E inside, then returns for Meera. I'm too terrified and ashamed to ask if she's alive or dead. Instead I pick up my axe, Bill-E's dropped sword, and the syringe — my right arm tingles fiercely where Dervish hit me, but I can use my hand now — and drop them in the back of the van beside the bodies. Dervish closes the door on the beast and the woman. Then we climb in up front and drive back to the mansion.

✠ For a full minute I say nothing, as if this is an ordinary drive home on a normal night. Dervish concentrates on the road, driving slowly for once in his life. His hands are shaking on the steering wheel. I watch him change gears. Then, unable to hold the questions back any longer, I spit it out.

"You knew Bill-E was a werewolf."

"Obviously."

"How long have you known?"

"A few months. Since he started wandering the forest in a daze around the time of a full moon, killing animals." His head turns briefly. "You know about that?"

"Yes. That's what put us on to you. Bill-E saw you collecting the bodies and getting rid of them in the incinerator."

Dervish winces. "By disposing of the kills, making sure nobody else found them, I hoped to avoid suspicion and protect him. Guess I was a little too smart for my own good."

I look back over the seat's headrest. I can see Bill-E and Meera. Meera's chest is rising and falling — she's alive. I study Bill-E's face. No hair. No fangs. But his skin's a darker shade than usual, his fingernails have sprouted, and his cheekbones have definitely changed shape — albeit slightly. And his eyes, if they were open, would be that eerie yellow color. And his mouth . . . those teeth . . .

"Why didn't you tell me?" I ask softly.

"That your best friend's a werewolf?" Dervish snorts.

"I'd have believed you if you'd shown me proof. I was ready to believe it about *you* — I could have believed it about Bill-E too."

"Perhaps," Dervish sighs. "But I hoped to spare you, the way I've spared Billy. I didn't know until tonight how damaging the change would be. Sometimes the madness touches us but passes. I was praying that he was merely moon-sick, that the disease was weak in him and wouldn't take hold."

Dervish drives in silence for a while, gathering his thoughts. I don't say anything, waiting for him to choose how to explain.

"How much of this have you guessed?" he asks eventually. "Tell me what you think you know."

"The Gradys are cursed," I answer directly. "Some of us turn into werewolves. It's been happening for centuries."

"Pretty good," Dervish commends me. "Only it goes back a lot further than centuries, and it's not just Gradys — it's the entire family line. What else?"

I shrug. "Not much. We thought you had the disease, but that you could control it, or at least lock yourself up when the moon was full."

"Nobody can control lycanthropy," Dervish says quietly. "When the disease takes hold — as it has in Billy tonight — you're doomed. The change takes a couple of months, but once the wolf comes to the fore, the human never resurfaces."

"You mean Bill-E's gone? He's . . ."

I can't continue. A terrible weight settles upon me.

"Not quite," Dervish says, and the weight lifts as suddenly as it fell into place.

"We can save him?" I ask, excited. "We can reverse the change?"

"There is a way," Dervish nods. "But we'll talk more about that later — and whether or not we wish to chance it."

"What do you mean?" I snap. "Of course we —"

"Your sister had the disease," Dervish interrupts softly. I stare at him, horrified. "To save Billy, we'll have to deal with Lord Loss, as your parents did. And if we do, we run the very real risk of winding up dead like them — Billy along with us."

"What does . . . *he* . . . have to do with this?" I croak.

"Later," Dervish says. "One mystery at a time. We're nearly home. Let's get Billy locked away safe and sound — then I'll tell you all about it."

✠ We pull up around back of the mansion, close to the tree stumps. Dervish turns off the engine and asks me to remove the sheet of corrugated iron and open the doors leading down to the secret cellar. He bundles the pair of unconscious bodies out of the back of the van while I'm doing that.

"Did you gain access this way or through the wine cellar?" he asks while I'm pulling the doors open.

"The wine cellar," I pant — the doors are heavy.

"Clever monkey," he chuckles. "You'll have to tell me about it — some other time. We have more pressing matters to deal with first." He picks Bill-E up and nods me forward.

Down the steps. Steep. Dark. Have to tread carefully, feeling for each stair.

"Do you need any help with Bill-E?" I ask over my shoulder.

"No," Dervish replies, coming down, blocking out the light of the moon. "I'll be fine. Dart ahead and light some extra candles."

I proceed to the bottom of the stairs, where I find a door. Pushing it open, I enter the cellar. Studying the entrance I've just come through, I note that the material on this side of the door is disguised to look like part of the wall, which is why I didn't spot it during my previous visit.

As I'm lighting candles on the main table — keeping as far clear of the Lord Loss folder as I can — Dervish stumbles in, goes to the cage, opens it with his left foot, and sets Bill-E down beside the deer. He makes sure Bill-E's comfortable, then locks the door and removes the key.

"Don't go anywhere near the cage when he wakes," Dervish says. "He'll howl like the devil, throw himself wildly at the bars — possibly injuring himself in the process — but steer clear, regardless. All he needs is a sliver of a chance to rip you open."

"I'll bear that in mind," I comment drily.

Dervish goes back up the steps and returns a minute later with Meera. He lays her down, smooths her hair back, stares at her bruised, motionless features.

"How is she?" I ask, dreading the answer.

"OK, I think," Dervish says, and my fear lessens. "But she'll be out for a while. He cracked her head hard on the pavement. We should get her to a doctor, have her checked over — but there isn't time. I'll take her to the house, out of harm's way, before . . . before we see to Billy. We'll just have to hope for the best after that."

Dervish stands, walks around behind the desk, and collapses into his chair, sighing deeply. He tells me to pull up one of the other chairs, but I prefer to stand — too nervous to sit.

"I want to know about werewolves," I tell him bluntly. "I want to know what Lord Loss has to do with them, and how you know Gret had it, and how we reverse it in Bill-E."

Dervish nods. "Reasonable questions. But I'm surprised you haven't asked the most obvious one — since this is a family disease, passed on from one generation to the next, how come Billy has it?"

"I know all about Bill-E's connection to our family," I huff.

Dervish stares at me, slack-jawed. "Care to tell me how?"

"Bill-E figured it out years ago. Like he said, it didn't take a genius to guess that you were his father. Now tell me about —"

"*What?*" Dervish yelps, jerking forward. "He thinks *I'm* his dad?"

"Of course." I frown. "Aren't you?"

Dervish sits back. Groans and shuts his eyes. "I'm a

horse's ass," he snarls. "I should have seen that coming. How can I have gone all these years . . ."

He clears his throat and levels his gaze on me. "Pull up a chair," he commands. "It sounds like a bad movie cliché, but you're going to want to sit down for this."

I start to come back with a sarcastic reply. Spot the steel in his eyes. Drag over a chair and sit opposite Dervish, like a student before a teacher.

"There's probably some diplomatic, sensitive, compassionate way to put this," Dervish says, "but one doesn't spring readily to mind, and I don't have time to go searching. So I'll put it plainly, no matter how upsetting it might be.

"I'm not Billy's father — I'm his uncle."

I stare at Dervish uncertainly. "I don't understand."

"People aren't perfect, Grubbs," he mutters. "Even the best of us make mistakes. Life's complicated. We all . . ." He clears his throat. "Your mother never liked me, and made no secret of the fact."

"What's that got to do with —" I start, but he silences me with a gesture.

"I visited Cal a few times over the years. She accepted that. But except for a single trip here years ago, she refused to step foot in Carcery Vale. So Cal used to come by himself. It was a serious bone of contention between them. I tried many times to talk to Sharon about it, but she wouldn't . . ."

Dervish trails off into a brooding silence, then begins again. "Your father loved your mother — and you and Gret — but he wasn't a saint. He traveled a lot, on business, alone — but he didn't always *sleep* alone."

I leap to my feet, furious at what Dervish is suggesting. But before I can lay into him, he continues quickly.

"They were one-night stands or short affairs. Meaningless. Sharon never found out — or so Cal told me. My brother had many admirable qualities, but fidelity wasn't one of them. He never wished to hurt your mother, but he couldn't remain true to her. It wasn't in his nature."

"Why are you telling me this?" I hiss, fingers clenched into fists, tears in my eyes.

Dervish looks at me sideways, as though I'm a fool for asking. "Because one year he had an affair with a Valer while he was staying with me. And the woman wound up pregnant. She didn't tell him about it until after the baby was born, and then refused all offers of his to get involved. Emily Spleen was headstrong, determined to live life her own way. She told Cal she wasn't —"

"Stop!" I gasp, stumbling back into my chair. "Don't," I beg.

"I took a vow early in life never to have children," Dervish says, ignoring my plea. "I was afraid the disease would take hold in them. I was determined not to put them — and myself — through that torment. Cal didn't share that view — he thought life was worth the risk.

"I looked after Billy when Emily died because he was my nephew — not because he was my son. Cal was Billy's father, Grubbs.

"Billy isn't your cousin — he's your *brother*."

THE CURSE

✠ ✠ ✠

A LONG silence. Wanting to roar at Dervish, call him a liar, make him take the words back. But there's no reason for him to lie about something like this. Nothing but sad honesty in his eyes.

Feeling sick. Instantly mad at Dad for what he did. But just as instantly glad — I'm not alone! I thought I lost everything when the demons attacked. Now I discover I have a brother.

"This is crazy," I moan, torn between rage and delight. "I don't know what to make of it. I can't handle it."

"Of course you can," Dervish snaps. "You handled the deaths of your parents and Gret — this is small fry in comparison."

"But . . . I always thought . . ." I shake my head, not sure what I'm thinking or what I feel. "Why didn't you tell Bill-E? You should have, especially after his Mom died. He could have come to live with us. Dad could —"

"Cal could do nothing!" Dervish barks. "Not without revealing the truth and tearing his family apart." He runs a hand through his short grey hair. "But he tried to do it anyway. He came here to claim Billy when Emily died, despite the havoc it would cause."

"Why didn't he?" I ask.

"Ma and Pa Spleen threatened legal action. He would have fought them in court, except he knew he'd lose — they'd simply point out to the judge that Emily hadn't told the boy who his father was, or allowed Cal access to him while she was alive. He hadn't a hope."

"Couldn't you have cast a spell on them — made them give Bill-E to him?"

"I'm not *that* powerful," Dervish chuckles humorlessly. "I 'persuaded' them to let me into Billy's life when Emily died, but that was as far as my influence ran."

I think it over some more, remembering Dad, how much he loved Mom, how happy they seemed together. I never suspected him of anything like this. I don't think Mom did either.

"I know it's a shock," Dervish says quietly, "but can I ask you to put it to one side for the moment? You've got the rest of your life to chew it over. Billy doesn't have the same luxury. If we don't act soon . . ."

I let out a long, shuddering breath. Glance at the unconscious boy — my brother! — in the cage, his dark skin and twisted hands. Recall the photos of the creatures in Dervish's lycanthropy books, warped and inhuman.

"OK. We'll discuss Dad later." I lean forward intently. "Tell me about werewolves."

✣ "I'll keep this as short as possible," Dervish says. Reaching under the table, he produces two cans of Coke from a drawer, hands one to me, and gulps thirstily at his. I sip mine while he speaks.

"The curse is ancient. We call it the Garadex curse, since the Garadexes were the first in our family to write about it. If other families have it, we don't know about them. Occasionally we'll hear of a stranger who's changed, but when we research their family tree we always find links to ourselves.

"Scientists who've studied the lycanthropic gene say it's a freak — they haven't found it anywhere else in nature. They don't know where it came from or why it functions the way it does."

He finishes his Coke, fishes out another, and continues. "We've kept the secret to ourselves. We're a large family, wealthy and powerful. Those of us unaffected by the disease protect the secret. That's why you and Billy aren't under observation in some scientific institute."

"Why would *I* be under observation?" I enquire. "I'm not a werewolf." I pause as a horrible thought strikes. *"Am I?"*

Dervish doesn't look at me. "I don't know," he answers softly. "The gene surfaces at random. Sometimes it strikes every member of a family branch, wiping them out. Other times it lies dormant for two or three generations. You're one of three children. Gret and Billy both succumbed to the disease. I wish I could say that makes you more or less likely to turn, but there's no way of guessing.

"The change strikes — *if* it strikes — anywhere between the ages of ten and eighteen. There have been a handful of cases involving younger children, but nobody past their teens has ever turned."

"That's why there are so many young faces in the hall of portraits!" I exclaim. "Those kids all turned into werewolves!"

Dervish nods glumly. "There's no known cure. Those who catch it are doomed to live as deranged animals for the rest of their days. They normally don't last long — twenty years at most, if allowed to live."

"What do you mean?"

Dervish taps the side of his can with his fingernails, a distant expression in his eyes. "It's a terrible curse," he says softly. "To see one you love change into an animal, to chain them up and endure their pain. . . . Many choose not to put themselves through the anguish. A lot of parents . . ." He stops tapping and his expression hardens. "They put them out of their misery."

I gulp dreadfully. "They *kill* them?"

He nods. "They're beasts," he says quickly before I can express my horror. "If they get loose, they kill. There are people in the family, a group called the Lambs, who handle the details if the parents can't. Family executioners, to be blunt."

"But you said there was a way to reverse it," I remind him, trying not to dwell on all those faces from the hall of portraits, the gruesome ends they must have endured.

"I'm coming to that," Dervish sighs. "Though be warned — when I tell you, you may wish that I hadn't."

A long pause. Then a groan from the cage — Bill-E stirring.

"When will he wake?" I ask, eyeing him nervously.

"Soon," Dervish says. "Let's go to my study — it won't be pretty when he starts bellowing."

"No," I mutter, gripping the edge of the table. "I want to be here for him."

Dervish nods understandingly, then returns to his story.

"Our scientists haven't been able to crack the wolfen gene and find a cure. But science isn't the only way to fight a disease. Magic works too."

Dervish reaches across the desk, roots through the books stacked to his left, and finds a thick tome. Opening it, he passes it to me, and I find myself gazing into the eyes of the family magician, Bartholomew Garadex.

"Old Bart devoted a large chunk of his life to trying to rid the family of its curse," Dervish says. "He believed it had its origins in magic. For decades he cast spells, experimented, and sought a cure in arcane volumes. But nothing worked. He could change a normal human's shape but could do nothing with a transformed werewolf. He was powerless, like everybody else.

"And then he met a creature who wasn't."

Dervish's face darkens. Taking the book from me, he closes it, then reaches for the folder where I found the drawing of Lord Loss.

"Stop!" I gasp. He looks at me questioningly. "I found that when I was here before," I tell him, eyeing the folder fearfully. "The drawing of Lord Loss spoke to me. Its lips and eyes moved."

"If I'd known you were so close to the truth," Dervish murmurs, "I would have warned you about that." He cocks a thumb at the door leading to the wine cellar. "As I told you, the house is safe. The land around is safe too. But I leave this cellar unprotected. There are times when I have to deal with entities not of this realm, and I need a base from which I can make contact."

Dervish runs a couple of fingers over the leather cover, contemplating it with an expression of equal parts respect, sadness, and fear. "Lord Loss can't cross the divide between his realm and ours uninvited," he says. "An ordinary person could look at that picture for decades without seeing anything untoward.

"But *you* aren't ordinary. You've faced demons and tapped into your magic potential — when you escaped through the dog flap. He was able to use your power to speak to you. He couldn't have harmed you through the book, but he might have been able to trick you into summoning him."

"But who — what! — is he?" I cry.

"Lord Loss is a demon master," Dervish says. "One of many supernatural beings who exist on the edges of our reality, in magical realms of their own. We call them the Demonata. Some meddle in the ways of humans, most have nothing to do with us, while a few — like Lord Loss — feed upon us."

My hands are trembling. I grip them tightly between my knees.

"Lord Loss is a sentinel of sorrow," Dervish says. "He feeds on human pain and suffering. A funeral is a three-course meal to him. A lonely, suicidal person's a tasty snack.

He delights in our fear and grief, encourages it when possible, then drains it and grows strong on humanity's weakness."

"How does he do it?" I croak. "How does he feed?"

"I'd have to get deep into metaphysics to explain that," Dervish snorts. "Let's just say he has a psychic straw through which he can suck a person's pain.

"Now, old Bart knew about Lord Loss — he'd seen him feeding on grieving members of the family — but he didn't care. Bartholomew was interested only in lifting the curse, not warding off demons. But later in life, he spent time studying the Demonata. They can live for thousands of years. I believe Bartholomew hoped to learn their secret. He never did, but at some point he found out that Lord Loss had the power to reverse the lycanthropic change."

"You mean Lord Loss can cure Bill-E?" I exclaim.

"If he chooses to."

"Then let's summon him!" I shout, leaping out of my chair. "What are we waiting for? Let's call him here now and —"

"The Demonata are evil and selfish," Dervish interrupts. "It's possible to strike deals with some of them, but they'll do nothing out of the goodness of their hearts — as you know, some don't even have a heart!"

"Then how . . . ?"

Dervish gestures for me to sit. I'm exasperated, but I obey.

"Bartholomew tried everything to get Lord Loss to help. He begged, he threatened, he even offered his soul."

"Souls are real?" I blurt out.

"Absolutely," Dervish nods fiercely. "And prized by demons above all other possessions. A soul can be tormented far worse than a body. If I was to lose my soul, my body would continue to function — but on auto-pilot. I'd be like a zombie, an empty shell, feeding, breathing, walking — but not thinking or feeling. Meanwhile, in the universe of the Demonata, my soul would be put through every kind of hell imaginable — and many that aren't!

"If Bartholomew had been a younger man, he might have been able to tempt Lord Loss. Trouble is, a soul's only good to a demon as long as the human lives. Old Bart was close to death. Lord Loss judged it an inadequate trade-off.

"But Bartholomew was stubborn. He pursued Lord Loss and braved the attacks of his familiars, suffering many wounds that hastened the hour of his death. But eventually old Bart discovered Lord Loss's great obsession, which he —"

Guttural roars drown Dervish out. Bill-E's on his feet, clutching the bars of the cage, shaking them, screaming, his face a dark mask of furious lines, teeth bared, tongue lashing wildly from side to side, his yellow eyes gleaming through the narrow slits of his eyelids.

"Bill-E!" I yell, jumping to my feet, stepping towards the cage.

"Easy," Dervish says, grabbing my arm. "Remember what I told you — he'll kill you if you get too close."

I stare numbly at Bill-E as he screams, pulls at the bars, kicks and head-butts them, his eyes all the time on Dervish and me.

"Does he recognize us?" I ask sickly.

"No," Dervish replies.

Bill-E quits wrestling with the bars and turns away, disgusted. He stumbles over the deer, which shakes fearfully. Bill-E stops and grins savagely. Circles the defenseless

beast, sniffing, growling. Then he falls on its neck. Claws —
teeth — ripping — blood.

My cheeks are wet. I'm crying again.

"Let's go," Dervish whispers. "We can finish this in my
study."

"I don't want to leave him alone," I sob.

"Werewolves don't get lonely," Dervish says. "They feel
only hunger and hate."

He picks up Meera and nudges me towards the door leading to the wine cellar. I pause at the exit. One last horrified
study of Bill-E Spleen — my brother. Then I follow my uncle to sanity.

THE CHALLENGE

✠ ✠ ✠

DERVISH lays Meera on one of the mansion's many beds. He examines her again, in more detail this time. He tries to wake her by calling her name and gently shaking her. When that fails he goes to the bathroom, comes back with a glass of water, uses his fingers to flick drops at her face. She doesn't stir.

Dervish steps away grimly. "I could try to bring her round with magic," he says, "but I'm not sure how serious the damage is. I could make it worse."

"Why don't you just leave her?" I ask. "She'll live, won't she?"

"I think so."

"Then let her sleep. That'll be best for her, right?"

Dervish stares at me, troubled, then walks out of the room without saying anything. I wrap a blanket over Meera, then close the door on her and head up to the study.

✠ ✠ ✠

✠ After the dark of the cellar, the study seems warmer and brighter than ever. I lose myself in a large leather chair, knees drawn up to my chest, head tucked between them, weary and afraid. Dervish is standing by a chess set. This is his favorite set, the pieces based on characters from *The Lord of the Rings*. Dervish picks up a brightly painted hobbit figurine and toys with it absently while he speaks.

"I don't think you've ever truly appreciated the complexities of chess," he says. "So few pieces, yet so many possibilities. No two games are ever the same. You can learn the rules in an afternoon, yet spend the rest of your life trying to master them."

"Stick chess up your ass!" I shout, coming alive with fury. "Bill-E's chained up in the cellar, twisted and insane. Meera's unconscious, maybe comatose. And all you can warble on about —"

"Lord Loss plays chess," Dervish interrupts quietly. "The Demonata are not, by nature, playful creatures, but he's an exception. I don't know where or when he acquired his hunger for the game, but by the time Bartholomew Garadex met him, he was a committed player, albeit one of limited experience."

"Where's this going?" I grumble, though I have an idea.

"When you walked in on your parents, did you notice any chess boards?"

Breathing thinly. Thinking back. The blood. Web-like walls. The demons. And, on the floor, scattered chess pieces, broken boards. Plus the gouged board in the study.

"Yes," I sigh.

Dervish talks swiftly. "Bartholomew played many games

with Lord Loss while trying to persuade him to help lift the curse. His familiars weren't allowed to pester Bartholomew at the chess board, so it was the safest way to conduct a conversation with Lord Loss. Over time he noticed that Lord Loss cared almost as much about chess as he did about feeding on humanity's sorrow.

"On a hunch, old Bart severed connections with the demon master and avoided him for several months. When he finally crossed the divide to the Demonata's universe again, Lord Loss was surly and irritable, eager to resume play.

"Bartholomew refused." Dervish chuckles drily. "It's dangerous, riling a demon. They can be abominable angels of destruction when offended. Lord Loss could have unleashed all of his familiars upon old Bart, which would have been —"

"He has others as well as Artery and Vein?" I snap.

"Oh yes," Dervish says. "They're just his current favorites. He has hundreds of familiars. If he'd sicced them on Bartholomew, they'd have torn him limb from limb, and all the magic in the world couldn't have repelled them.

"But, as old Bart had gambled, Lord Loss didn't send the demons in. As intense as his anger was, his fascination with chess proved stronger. Instead of crushing Bartholomew, he whined and complained and tried to bargain. So Bartholomew struck for gold. He told Lord Loss he wouldn't play unless the demon master lifted the curse of the Garadexes.

"No bite. Chess was an obsession, but it wasn't *that* precious to him. So old Bart tried another approach. He proposed a series of contests in which he'd play for the lives of individual family members. After lengthy discussions, they agreed to stage a number of matches, best of five games per match. For each match that Bartholomew won, Lord Loss would cure a Garadex. But if Bartholomew ever lost, Lord Loss would take possession of his soul.

"And so the contests commenced, two or three games per week — Lord Loss set the rate. According to Bartholomew's records, Lord Loss hated losing. Like most of the Demonata, he's despisingly proud. They consider themselves superior to humans, and to lose to one — at anything — is a great disgrace.

"Yet lose he did." Dervish chuckles throatily. "Bartholomew gave his time over entirely to chess, playing for hours on end each day and night, with the best opponents he could find, learning, and improving. He lost six games in the first three months — then never again. He hit a fifty-nine-game winning streak, which showed no sign of ending.

"And then he died."

Dervish shrugs. "He was old, and his earlier battles with Lord Loss's familiars had drained him. It was peaceful in the end — he passed away in his sleep."

"What happened then?" I ask, absorbed in the story.

"For a long time, nothing," Dervish says. "Nobody in our family knew of Bartholomew's matches with Lord Loss. He never told them how he was affecting the cures. Several Garadexes were witches and wizards, but they were unable to unlock the secrets of his diaries, which he'd encoded with strong spells.

"Eventually, almost forty years after the great magician's death, Davey McKay — a distant relative who'd lost four of his five children to the curse — decoded the diary and discovered the demonic secret. He immediately contacted Lord

Loss in an attempt to renew the contests and reverse the change in his youngest child, who was just starting to change.

"The demon master was slow to respond. Bartholomew had humiliated him. He was wary of suffering another string of defeats at the hands of a human. Also, Davey wasn't a magician — his soul was of only minor interest to Lord Loss. But Davey was resourceful. He sought a twist to spike Lord Loss's imagination, a challenge that would appeal to his warped sensibilities."

Dervish lapses into a thoughtful silence. He's still playing with the hobbit chess piece. With his free hand, he pulls open a drawer and takes out a photo. Slides it across the desk. I look — Mom, Dad, Gret, and me. A snapshot taken on one of Dad's birthdays.

"Davey's solution was dreadful," Dervish says as I stare at the photo, "but it had to be. Lord Loss wasn't interested in anything less. The rules he proposed were — one match, best of five games, like before. If Davey won, his son would have his humanity restored, and both would be free. But if Lord Loss won, he could kill both Davey *and* the child.

"Lord Loss was keen on Davey's idea, but he added a few kinks of his own. When playing Bartholomew, he'd told his familiars to stand at bay. He refused to grant Davey that privilege. Somebody would have to partner Davey and fight the demons while he played. As long as Davey's protector lived, the familiars wouldn't attack Davey. But if his partner was killed they'd be free to slaughter Davey and his son too.

"Another new rule was that the games had to be played simultaneously, in a single sitting — to heap the pressure on Davey and his partner.

"And his final clause — if Davey won, he'd have to enter Lord Loss's realm and fight him personally for possession of his soul."

"What?" I mutter, not catching the meaning of the last part.

"The games take place between the Demonata's universe and ours," Dervish explains. "You probably noticed in your parents' room that there were bits of our world as well as bits of Lord Loss's. That in-between state was where Davey would challenge Lord Loss. If Davey won, his son would be cured, and the boy and Davey's partner could get on with their lives. But Davey would have to enter Lord Loss's world and fight the demon master on his home turf. If he beat him, he'd walk free. But if he lost, Lord Loss would take control of his soul, and he'd live out his remaining days as a zombie."

"Sounds like a raw deal to me," I grunt.

"It was," Dervish agrees. "But those were the terms. Davey had to agree." Dervish pauses, then says softly, "Davey McKay lost. His brother stood as his partner. The demons overwhelmed him. Davey was killed before even one of the games was decided. His son too. All three were ripped to pieces by the demons."

He takes the photo from me and gazes at it in heavy silence.

"But Davey's sacrifice wasn't in vain," he resumes. "Lord Loss developed a taste for this new contest. He approached Davey's relatives — those with magical powers — offering them the chance to compete for lives as Davey had.

"Most refused. But two — both with young children on the verge of turning — accepted the challenge. One was defeated — but the other won. His victory gave hope to the others, and a series of Garadexes and Gradys have sustained the challenge over the long decades since. Some win, some lose. Most who win subsequently lose their souls in the ensuing battle in Lord Loss's realm, but a few have made the journey back, proof that it can be done."

Dervish lays the photo back in the drawer and closes it slowly. He blinks owlishly and wipes a hand across his eyes — he's fighting back tears.

"Your parents didn't win," he says. "Gret was infected. Your father and mother challenged Lord Loss. One of them proved inadequate to the task. All three died as a result. I was meant —"

His voice catches and he turns away, rubbing his eyelids, trembling with emotion. "Your father and I had an agreement," he says bleakly. "If any of his children succumbed to the disease, I was to be his partner. I thought he was wrong to have children, but I loved him, and I loved the kids he fathered. I wasn't going to stand to one side in their hour of need."

"Then why weren't you there?" I cry, tears streaming down my cheeks.

"He never told me Gret was changing," he croaks. "Your mother must have convinced him to let *her* face the demons with him. I'm sure Sharon had Gret's best interests at heart, but I was a better chess player, and a much stronger fighter. Cal should have held me to my promise. He should have called. Maybe I could have . . ."

He breaks down. His eyes close. His hands clench into fists. Then he raises his face to the ceiling and howls. From the secret cellar I imagine I hear an echoing howl, as the transformed Bill-E Spleen pauses during feeding and answers his uncle's tortured call.

✠ I stop crying before Dervish does. I don't think he cries very often, so he has a hard time regaining control. When the tears finally cease and he's wiping his face clean with a denim sleeve, I put an accusation to him as softly as I can. "Are you saying it was Mom's fault?"

"Of course not!" he answers promptly.

"But if Dad had picked you instead of her . . ."

Dervish hesitates, choosing his words carefully. "I've got to be truthful — I was the logical choice. But logic and magic don't always mix. Sometimes amateurs fare better than professionals. Nobody ever really knows how they'll fare until they put themselves on the spot."

He pulls out a handkerchief and blows his nose. "In the end, it's all relative. Your father chose — rightly or wrongly — and the outcome stands. We can't change the past and we'd be fools if we tried.

"But whatever my personal feelings about his choice," Dervish adds, "don't ever think I believe it was your mother's fault. It wasn't. It was *our* curse, not hers. She deserves nothing short of absolute love and respect for taking on that curse, and laying her life on the line to try and avert it."

I nod slowly, thinking it over. "But if they *hadn't* laid their lives on the line," I whisper. "If they'd called in the Lambs and not gone to Lord Loss . . ."

"They'd be alive." Dervish says it bluntly. "That's why I said you might not like the truth. They put Gret's life before their own — and yours. If they hadn't interfered, you'd have lost a sister but kept your parents."

I stare at him uncertainly, my lower lip trembling, part of me hating Mom and Dad for putting me through this, another part hating Gret, blaming her for the mess.

Dervish reads my thoughts and shakes his head calmly. "Don't go down that road, Grubbs," he says. "Cal and Sharon did what they had to. They'd have done the same for you if you'd been infected. I know you feel cheated. I know you want them back. But if you look deep inside, and recall the people they were, the love they had for you and Gret, you'll understand why they did it."

"They should have told me," I moan. "They cut me out completely. I could have helped. I —"

"No," Dervish says firmly. "The rules are clear — only two may challenge Lord Loss and his familiars. Telling you would have achieved nothing."

"It would have prepared me for the worst," I disagree.

"I don't think they wanted to think about that," Dervish sighs. "Doubts have a way of eating a person from the inside out. Most who face Lord Loss choose not to focus on all that can go wrong, because it makes it more likely that something *will* go wrong."

"But —" I begin.

"Grubbs," Dervish interrupts curtly, "we can sit here arguing all night. But that won't bring your parents and Gret back. And it won't help Billy. Letting go isn't easy, but you have to forget about your parents for a while. If you can't, you're no good to me."

"'No good to you'?" I echo, frowning. "What are you talking about? What do you want me to do?"

Dervish leans forward, his features impassive. "I want you to be my second," he says. "I want you to stand by my side and battle Vein and Artery while I challenge Lord Loss at chess."

The world goes numb.

THE CHOICE

✠ ✠ ✠

"YOU'RE loco!" I scream. "Sheer bloody nuts!"

"I'm many things," Dervish answers calmly, "but I don't think I'm crazy."

"You must be! Only a crazy man would ask a kid to fight a couple of demons!"

Dervish studies me quietly, then gets to his feet and picks up his *Lord of the Rings* chess set. He heads for the door.

"Where are you going?" I snap, lurching in front of him, blocking the way.

"I'm taking this down to the cellar," he says. "I need to have five sets in place before I summon Lord Loss — each game is played on a separate board."

"Didn't you hear me?" I hiss. "I won't do it! I'm not —"

"Grubbs," he silences me with a smile. "It's OK. I asked. You refused. That's the end of it. It was a request, not a command."

I glare at him suspiciously. "It was?"

He nods. "There are others who can help. One of my

friends is a near grandmaster. He'll face Lord Loss. I'll handle Vein and Artery." He nods at a plain chess board to my left. "But I'd be obliged if you'd help me carry the sets down."

My eyes narrow. "If you're trying to trick me . . ."

"No tricks," he says, and I believe him. Getting out of his way, I pick up the board and follow him out of the room.

✠ Down the stairs to the main hall. Taking our time, careful not to drop any pieces. Thinking hard about what Dervish said.

"If you've got friends who can help," I mutter, "why ask me?"

"Billy's your brother," Dervish replies. "I thought you might want to be part of this."

"But it doesn't make sense," I press. "You need the best person for the job. Why offer it to me?"

"Ideally I want to face Lord Loss with someone who's proved their courage and ability under fire," he says. "Someone who's faced a demon and lived. I only personally know six people who've done that. Meera was one of them. But she can't do it now."

"What about the others?"

"Four of them are currently out of contact."

He reaches the door to the cellar and stops talking while he opens it with his elbows. Silence as we descend. I wait until we're at the wine rack that hides the entrance to the secret passageway before asking, "And the sixth?"

"*You're* the sixth," he says, stepping forward into darkness.

✠ ✠ ✠

✠ The secret cellar. Five chess sets lie in place on the three tables, which we've shoved together, piling the books and other odds and ends on the floor. Dervish is lining up the pieces, making sure they're in the right places. Bill-E's still chewing on the deer carcass. He spits and snarls at us every so often.

Dervish hasn't said anything since our trip down with the first two boards. We've worked silently, carting in the boards and pieces, clearing the tables and rearranging them. It's only now, while I watch him adjust the pieces, that I work up the courage to broach the subject again.

"I still don't understand why you want me to help. Why not wait for Meera to recover? You don't have to stage the contest tonight, do you?"

"No," Dervish says. "But waiting's dangerous. Lord Loss can reverse the change, even in one who's been a werewolf for several years. But often the mind can't be restored. Every day we wait drives Bill-E closer to the point from which it's not worth bringing him back.

"Besides," he adds, "how would we explain his absence to his grandparents, teachers, the police? We're in the middle of an unreal adventure, but we're still part of the real world. Try telling a cop you've got a boy locked up in a cage because he's a werewolf — see where it lands you!"

"I didn't think of that." I manage a sick smile, which quickly fades. "I'm just a kid," I say quietly. "I wouldn't be any good to you."

Dervish wipes a spot of dust from the head of a king. "You've fought demons and lived to tell the tale. You've tapped into your magic potential. You can fight them on their own terms — even if you are just a kid," he adds with a grin.

"I *want* to help," I groan. "I'd do almost anything to get Bill-E out of the hell he's in. But I saw Artery work Gret like a puppet, and —"

"Don't beat yourself up over it," Dervish interrupts kindly. "You're under no obligation. You came here to recover, not get dragged deeper into a nightmare. I shouldn't have asked. And I wouldn't have, except . . ."

He doesn't finish, so I say it for him. ". . . except you need me."

He shrugs. "Like I said, there's a friend I can call. But I'd rather have you. If I told you anything else, I'd be a liar."

✠ Studying Bill-E as Dervish fetches weapons. His face and hands red with the deer's blood. Patting his stomach. Smiling jaggedly. Gazing at me through unnatural yellow eyes.

Thinking about Lord Loss. Recalling the ferocious power and speed of Artery and Vein. Fearing for my uncle's and brother's lives.

Dervish enters with a small axe, a mace, and a sword. Lays them on the floor with the others he's already installed. Part of the rules — he can use as many weapons as he pleases.

"Would you want me to play chess or fight?" I ask, wishing I could keep my mouth shut.

"I've seen you play," Dervish says. "No offense, but you'd have to fight — Lord Loss would crush you on the chess boards."

"But you'd stand a better chance against Vein and Artery

than me," I counter. "You're stronger and experienced. I know nothing about weapons or magic."

"You don't have to," Dervish says. "The magic knows you. That's what matters. You tapped into your potential when you faced the demons before. You'd tap into it again. Instinct."

"But you're the logical choice," I insist. "You'd be better than me."

Dervish nods somberly. "Probably."

"And your friend's better at chess than me. So you fighting and him playing is the ideal partnership. Right?"

Dervish looks at me curiously. "You don't have to talk yourself out of this," he says. "You've said you don't want to do it and I've accepted your decision."

"But I feel lousy!" I cry. "Like I'm letting you down!"

"You're not," Dervish says. "Ability and potential mean nothing if the will to compete isn't there."

"But even if I *had* the will, you'd still be better off with the other guy, wouldn't you?" I press, hoping he'll agree.

Dervish shakes his head and doesn't answer.

✠ The room where Meera lies unconscious. Dervish tries again to wake her. Again he fails. He returns to his study, rubbing the back of his neck. Sitting behind his desk, he runs his fingers over a phone book. "Time to call my friend," he says, glancing up at me. "Final chance to change your mind, Grubbs."

I don't say a word.

Dervish opens the book and searches for a number.

"Pablo should be here within a few hours. You can go stay in the Vale if you want, but you don't need to. You'll be safe here. The demons won't be able to leave the cellar."

I don't reply. Thinking of the battle to come. Filled with shame.

"If Pablo and I defeat Lord Loss and his familiars, but I lose the one-on-one fight later," Dervish continues, "you'll have to take care of me."

"What?" I mumble.

"My body will survive if I lose the battle after the chess match," he explains, "but my soul and mind won't. I'll be able to move about, but I won't be capable of thought or speech. I won't be able to shop, pay bills, cook, clean the house, etc. You'll have to babysit me, or hire somebody to do it."

Dervish taps a drawer in his desk. "The necessary forms and information sheets are here. Names and numbers of lawyers and bankers, details of various credit accounts. You have my permission — written as well as verbal — to manage my estate as you see fit, though a large portion will remain in the hands of your legal guardians until you come of age."

"I don't want your money," I sniff.

"You won't feel that way always," he smiles. Picks up the phone. Hesitates. Lays it down. "One last thing. If things pan out badly. I'll appear no better than a mindless robot. You might feel sorry for me, be tempted to put me out of my misery."

"I wouldn't do that!" I shout. "I'm not a killer! I couldn't —"

"You could," Dervish cuts me short. "Most people are capable of extreme actions when pushed." He licks his lips nervously. "You mustn't. Time is different in the Demonata's universe. There's no telling how long our fight could last. The few who've fought him and returned have been absent for months . . . years . . . on one occasion, decades.

"No matter how much time passes, there's always hope," he says. "Don't give up on me, Grubbs. Look after my body. I might have need of it again someday."

He finds the number in the book, picks up the phone, and starts dialing.

"Wait," I stop him. He looks up expectantly. I lick my lips nervously. "What happens if you don't win and *I* turn into a werewolf later?"

Dervish's features soften. "'And the wolf shall lie down with the lamb.'"

"Come again?" I frown.

"It's a biblical quote. Isaiah. It's where the Lambs got their name from." He jerks his head at the desk. "There's a black folder in the second drawer down on the left. Names and numbers for the Lambs. Contact them if the need arises. But only do it if you're *sure* that you're changing. The Lambs don't mess around. Once you set them in motion, they won't stop, even if you change your mind and try to call them off."

"How will I know?" I ask. "Bill-E didn't know he was changing."

Dervish chews on his lower lip in thoughtful silence, then says, "Nobody turns without warning. If the lycanthropy strikes, there'll be at least two or three full moons during which you won't physically alter, but run wild like Bill-E did. You won't be able to recall such episodes, but if you find blood under your fingernails, animal hairs between your teeth . . ."

Dervish stiffens and speaks roughly. "That's when you need to think about calling in the Lambs."

As I stare at him miserably, Dervish returns his attention to the phone and hits the buttons. The phone at the other end rings and is picked up almost instantly. I hear a man say, "Yes?"

Dervish starts to reply.

"Tell him it's OK," I interrupt softly. "Tell him you rang his number by accident."

"Grubbs, you don't have to —"

"I won't live with the threat of the change hanging over me. Or with the guilt of not fighting for Bill-E." Deep breath. Thinking — crazy for doing this. But also — it's what Dad would have wanted.

"I'll do it," I wheeze. "I'll fight Vein and Artery." The thinnest, most fleeting of smiles. Mock bravado. Grubbs Grady — demon killer! "I'm your man."

THE SUMMONING

�֍   ✦   ✦

THE cellar. Bill-E beating at the bars of his cage with a bloody leg he's torn from the deer, howling madly. Dervish checking the chess boards and weapons, ignoring Bill-E. I want him to talk me out of it, tell me it's madness, reject my offer.

But he says nothing. In the study, he didn't even ask if I was sure, just nodded once and told Pablo he'd call him some other time. Then it was straight back here. No "Thank you," or "Well done, Grubbs," or "I'm proud of you."

I examine the chess boards with forced interest, desperate to keep my mind off the weapons. Five boards, laid in a line across the three tables. The *Lord of the Rings* set in the center, flanked by a board of crystal pieces on one side and Incan-fashioned pieces on the other. The sets at either end are ordinary.

"Did you lay the boards out that way for a reason?" I ask Dervish.

"No," he replies, testing a sword's handle, wiping it clean. "The sets don't matter, as long as there are five."

"Explain how the contest works," I urge him.

"The games are played simultaneously," Dervish says without looking over. "When it's my turn, I can move any piece I like, on any board. Lord Loss can then reply to the piece I've moved, or move a piece on a different board."

"That must be confusing."

"Yes. But it's confusing for him too." Dervish holds an axe up to the light of a thick candle and squints, judging the sharpness of its blade. "Lord Loss is an accomplished player, and he's had centuries to work on his game, but he has no supernatural advantage. If I keep my head, focus on the moves, and don't lose my nerve, I'll stand a fair chance."

"What sort of chance do *I* stand against Artery and Vein?" I ask.

Dervish looks at me coldly — then whips his arm forward and sends the axe flying straight at me!

Instant reaction — I spin — my left hand flies out — my fingers close around the axe handle mid-air — I arc it down, taking the speed out of it — then raise it high to defend myself, heart racing, confused and afraid.

Then I see my uncle's grin.

Breathing hard, I stare at Dervish, then at the axe in my hand.

"*That* sort," he says.

✠ "I still don't know how I caught it," I grumble, as Dervish searches among his books for a particular volume.

"You don't have to know," Dervish says. "It's magic." He

pauses and looks up at me. "Your instincts have been sharpened by your previous encounter with the demons. Obey those instincts. Let Vein and Artery set the tone and pace of the battle. React. Don't think. Suspend the laws of reality completely."

Dervish returns his attention to the books, finds the one he's after, flicks it open, and stands. "Make your inexperience work for you," he says. "You can't out-plan or out-think the demons. So don't try. Just go with the flow."

"You make it sound easy."

"It certainly won't be easy! But if you switch your brain off, you'll be amazed by what your body can do."

Dervish lays the book on the floor, bends over it, and reads a passage, running a finger over the words, muttering softly.

"What are you doing?" I ask.

"Several spells must be cast to open a window between Lord Loss's world and ours," Dervish says. "I have to make sure it's a small gateway — we don't want other demons following him through."

"That can happen?"

"Sure. The Demonata are always eager to cross the divide and wreak havoc. They'll seize any opening that presents itself."

"But don't you know the spells already?" I frown. "I thought you summoned him before."

"I did," Dervish nods. "Several times. But some spells are best not memorized."

He finishes the paragraph and closes the book. Walks to the wall to his left and lays both hands on it. "I'm starting now," he says, "but it'll be twenty minutes, maybe half an hour before the window opens. Stay close to the tables. Relax. Don't distract me."

While I lean against a table, nervously tapping and scratching at the wood, Dervish mutters arcane words at the wall, drawing signs upon it with his fingers. After a few minutes, steam seeps from the rough stone. Dervish leans into the steam, inhales, turns, and breathes out.

A shadowy bat flies from his mouth and flits across the cellar. I duck instinctively, even though it's nowhere near me. When I look again, the bat has vanished and Dervish has moved on to another patch of wall.

✠ Fifteen minutes into the summoning. All the walls are steaming. The air of the cellar is moist and hot, like in a sauna. Bill-E makes deep choking noises and flaps at the air with blood-red hands. Dervish has been breathing out a variety of smoky creatures — bats, snakes, dogs, insects. As I watch, he turns and exhales his largest yet — a full-sized wolf.

Bill-E gibbers wildly at the sight. Hisses at it, then ducks to the rear of his cage and crouches low, whimpering, as the spirit wolf floats towards him, evaporating before it touches the bars.

At any other time I'd feel pity for the poor beast Bill-E has become, but right now there's only room in my heart for terror.

✠ ✠ ✠

✠ Dervish steps away from the walls at last, eyes closed, face contorted. Walks directly to the folder containing the Lord Loss drawings. Picks it up and clutches it to his chest.

"This is where things get weird," he mutters, as steam pours from the walls and transparent worms drift in and out of his mouth.

"I can't wait," I half-laugh, almost hysterical.

"Whatever happens, don't scream," Dervish says. "We're at our most vulnerable while I'm searching the various portals for the one that connects with Lord Loss's realm. A scream could attract the interest of other demons — and that might be the end of us."

"We'll probably end on a grisly note anyway," I say gloomily.

"Perhaps," Dervish agrees. "But there are worse demons than Lord Loss."

My thoughts threaten to spin out of control as I try to imagine anything worse than Lord Loss. Then Dervish spreads his arms and barks a loud command, and the world dissolves around me.

✠ Walls and ceiling fading. Infinite space . . . a scattering of stars . . . meteors streak across the sky. But this space isn't black — it's red. An unending sky of redness, encircling the cellar like the drapes of hell.

The temperature escalates off the scale. Some of Dervish's books burst into flame and incinerate instantly. The bars of Bill-E's cage glow from the heat. All the candles in the cellar melt to the wick.

I check my clothes and hair, expecting flames, but although I can feel the terrible heat, it isn't burning me. Dervish and Bill-E aren't harmed either. Nor are the chess sets.

"Why aren't we toast?" I cry. The words come out as a croak — my mouth and throat are unbelievably dry.

"Protected," Dervish wheezes in reply, then lays a finger to his lips and shakes his head — no more speaking. He points to a meteor screaming across the sky overhead. As I gaze up, I realize it isn't a meteor — it's some enormous, incomprehensible, reality-defying monster!

Dervish squats and places both palms on the floor, which ripples beneath his touch, as if made of water. Muttering some spell — or prayer — he turns in a circle. His eyes are yellow when I next catch sight of his face, his teeth sharp and grey.

I open my mouth to scream — remember his warning — shut my lips quickly.

Dervish continues turning, and when he faces me again he looks normal. Standing, he picks up one of the unburnt books, flicks it open, and starts singing. Long, complicated words. His voice unnaturally clear and beautiful.

The red sky shimmers, then darkens as Dervish sings. I lose sight of the stars and meteor-monsters. The room slips into a hot, fearful blackness — no candles to shed any light. The last thing I see — Dervish, eyes closed, singing as though his life depended on it.

✠ I feel alone in the darkness, though I know by Dervish's singing and Bill-E's grunts and whines that I'm not.

Whistling sounds around me. Something long and silky brushes against my cheeks. I swipe at it, terrified — nothing there.

Dervish stops singing. The sudden silence is as disorienting as the lack of light.

"Dervish?" I whisper, not wishing to distract him, but needing to know he's still there.

"It's OK, Grubbs," comes his voice. "Don't move."

"It's dark," I note redundantly.

"We'll have all the light we care for soon enough," he promises.

An object brushes my left ear. I flinch. "There's something in the room with us!" I hiss.

"Yes," Dervish says. "Take no notice. Stand your ground."

It isn't easy, but I obey my uncle's order. The whistling sounds increase in volume, and I'm struck in various places by what feels like thick strands of rope. I wince and rub at my flesh, but otherwise don't react.

Gradually I notice a dull grey glow all around me, which grows in strength, illuminating the distorted cellar. The walls have been replaced by thick strands of cobwebs, which stretch away, layer after layer, apparently endless. Many of the strands are stained with blood. Some are as thick as a tree trunk, while others are as thin as a line of thread.

From one of the strands hang the severed heads of Mom, Dad, and Gret.

I can't hold back the scream, but Dervish anticipated this. He slides behind me and clamps both hands over my mouth.

I howl into the flesh of his palms, wild, sobbing, reaching for the heads, while at the same time trying to back away from them.

"They aren't real, Grubbs," Dervish grunts, struggling to contain me. "They're illusions. Let your fear go and they'll vanish."

I thrash more wildly in response. Can't think straight. The heads seem to be growing. Eyes huge, filled with sadness and pain. Mom's lips move silently. Gret sticks her tongue out at me — it's alive with maggots.

"They're testing you!" Dervish growls, fingers tightening over my lips. My neck's strained almost to snapping point. "If they can drive you insane, I'll have nobody to protect me from Artery and Vein!"

The names of the demons penetrate. Fighting the terror, I stare at the faces of my parents and sister, and spot minor mistakes — Dad's nose bends to the wrong side, Gret's hair shouldn't be that long, Mom's eyebrows are too thick.

I stop shaking. Lower my hands. Dervish releases me, but stays close, ready to gag me if I start screaming again.

"How do I make them go away?" I moan.

"Show you're not afraid," Dervish says. "Look at them without flinching."

"It's hard."

"I know. For me too. But you can do it, Grubbs. You have to."

Deep breaths. Exerting control. I lift my eyes and train them on the three heads dangling in front of me. Their features twist. Mom and Gret hiss at me hatefully. I don't look away.

Under the strength of my gaze, the heads disintegrate, melting like the candles. The web vibrates. The air bubbles. The molten waxy flesh of the heads rises, twisting, forming itself into three new shapes. A crocodile-headed dog. A murderous baby. And their master — Lord Loss.

"It begins," Dervish sighs, and steps forward to confront the demons.

THE BATTLE

✚ ✚ ✚

DERVISH stops at the place where the floor gives way to webs, spreads his arms, and shouts something unintelligible. Blue flames crackle from the tips of his fingers. He brings his hands together, then touches a thick strand of web. Blue fire runs up the thread to where it connects with another. Like lightning it streaks from strand to strand, arcing ever closer to Lord Loss and his familiars. Lord Loss shows no sign of fear. When the blue flame reaches him, it sizzles and hisses around him, but he only smiles and waves a hand, and the flame sputters out.

Lord Loss stretches his arms above his head. As he does, six other arms unfold from around his body, three on either side. No fingers, just mangled lumps of flesh at the ends. The demon master grips two strands, one with either set of hands, and climbs towards us like a grotesque spider. Vein and Artery follow close behind their master, Vein yapping, Artery snapping his teeth.

Studying the demons with terror. So many details I'd

forgotten. The tiny mouths in Artery's palms, the fact that he doesn't have a tongue in any mouth, the writhing cockroaches on his head, the fierceness of the flames burning in his empty eye sockets. Vein's tiny cruel eyes, her long leathery snout, bits of flesh caught between her teeth, the sleekness of her canine coat, female hands instead of paws. And Lord Loss — red skin stained with blood that oozes from hundreds of thousands of ragged cracks, his strange dark red eyes, and the hole where his heart should be, filled with writhing, hissing snakes.

The demons come to the end of the web and hesitate, swaying on a thin strand like evil vultures on a vine. Dervish stands beneath them, cool as a chunk of ice, hands pressed together.

"Hello, Dervish," Lord Loss says, his voice even sadder than I remembered. "It is good to see you again, my doomed friend."

"Good to see you also," Dervish replies tightly. Vein snaps at him, trying to frighten him, but Dervish only sniffs with disinterest.

"And my younger friend, poor Grubitsch Grady." Lord Loss sighs, subjecting me to his eerie red gaze. "Your sorrow is still strong. So sweet." His face wrinkles and blood seeps from cracks on both cheeks. He licks the blood from his flesh with an inhumanly long tongue, then extends a hand. "Come to me, Grubitsch. Let me feed on your pain. Misery should be celebrated, not endured. In my world you will be an emperor of suffering. Be mine, Grubitsch. Turn your back on this insane challenge and accept your true destiny."

I find myself sneering, and without meaning to, I draw

myself up straight, glare openly at the demon lord, and snap, "Stick it up your crack, you warped son of a mutant bitch!"

Lord Loss's face drops. Vein and Artery gibber furiously. Dervish laughs.

"You will pay for that insult," Lord Loss snarls, eyes glowing, blood flowing.

"Only if we lose," Dervish chuckles. "You can't touch him if we win."

"Oh, but Dervish, you won't win," Lord Loss says, his voice reverberating with gloominess. "I wish there was hope — you remind me of Bartholomew Garadex, a most rare human. But you must face facts — this night you die. The boy is weak, unfit for such a challenge."

"Don't listen to him," Dervish warns me. "He's trying to make you think you're lost before you start."

"I know what he's up to — it won't work," I grunt. But inside I'm not so cocky. There's such sadness in the demon's voice and eyes. Is it true? Are we destined to lose?

"One final chance, Grubitsch," Lord Loss whispers. "Give yourself to me now and you can avoid the terror and agony. Your death will not be quick, but it will be pleasurable. Your mother, at the end, wished she had accepted my offer. She begged to serve me, but it was too late."

"I don't believe you," I say evenly. "Mom would never have begged a piece of scum like you for anything — even her life!"

Lord Loss's eyes narrow. "A second insult," he murmurs. "You shall not make a third." He faces Dervish. "I tire of these vain human posturings. I came to play chess. Are you ready?"

"Yes."

"Who will take to the boards with me?"

"I will."

Lord Loss lays a hand over his mouth to cover a small smile. "The boy is to fight Vein and Artery? I am astonished. I assumed Grubitsch was a chess maverick who would pit his wits against mine. But to throw him into combat with my savage familiars . . ."

"Grubbs will be fine," Dervish says, but his voice doesn't ring with confidence.

"So be it," Lord Loss sighs. "I would have rather fought a noble contest, but if you are to play into our hands, there is nothing for it but to sweep to a swift victory and make a quick end of you."

Lord Loss lowers himself off of the web and hovers just in front of Dervish, the jagged strips of flesh at the ends of his legs never touching the ground. Six of his arms fold around his ribs, leaving the upper pair free. Blood drips from his body and sizzles when it hits the stones of the floor.

Dervish steps aside and points to the chess boards. Lord Loss drifts towards them, lips splitting into the closest he can get to a genuinely warm smile. He circles the tables, running his fingers over some of the chess pieces. On the web, Vein and Artery snap and spit, scratching impatiently at the silky strands, hungry for battle and blood.

"I hope you prove more worthy an opponent than your brother, Dervish," Lord Loss says spitefully. "He was on the back foot from the fourth move. It was quite embarrassing, the ease with which he succumbed. I think, deep down, he secretly wished to lose — just as Grubitsch does."

"Shut up!" I yell, taking an angry step towards him, hands clenched into fists.

"Easy, Grubbs," Dervish mutters. "He's trying to goad you. Ignore his crap. Clear your mind. Focus on the fight."

"Wise advice," Lord Loss nods. "But Grubitsch is unable to heed it. He is full of fire and fury — like his mother. Her failures proved to be your father's downfall. He might have fared better had he not been so worried about her, just as Dervish is worried about you. What will you say to your uncle when you fail him, Grubitsch? How will you apologize for —"

"If this continues," Dervish interrupts softly, "the game's off." Lord Loss stares at him archly. "I'm not bluffing. Let it be a fair contest, me against you, Grubbs against your slaves, or there'll be no contest at all."

"You would sacrifice the wretched Billy Spleen so cheaply?" Lord Loss smirks.

"If I have to," Dervish says, and his face is stone.

Lord Loss studies my uncle in troubled silence, then shrugs and sits on the side of the chess boards behind the black pieces. "Very well. We shall dispense with the pleasantries. Take your place, Dervish Grady, and face your finish."

Dervish walks across to me. Grips my shoulders. Stares hard into my eyes. "You know what you have to do," he says. "Fight hard and dirty — to the death."

"Piece of cake," I grin weakly. "Good luck."

"We make our own luck tonight," he says in reply. He releases me and marches to the chess boards. Sits, takes a breath, then without any formalities reaches forward, grips a pawn on the middle board, and moves it forward.

Immediately, Vein and Artery leap from the web and zone in on me, screeching, snarling, the stench of death thick in the air about them.

✠ No time to check Lord Loss's response to Dervish's opening move. I toss myself wildly to the left. Vein shoots overhead, crocodile jaws snapping together on thin air, human fingers wriggling.

Artery lands on my back. His left hand grabs my neck. Teeth bite into my flesh. I howl and roll over, seeking to squash the hell-child. He leaps free before I complete the move, chuckling darkly.

In the cage, Bill-E roars and shakes the bars, sensing the threat of the demons even in his beastlike form.

Vein attacks again, bounding across the floor. My right hand snakes out. Fingers open. An axe jumps into my palm from the pile of weapons several meters away. I sit up and throw. It arcs towards Vein. Bounces hard off her snout. Only a scratch, but the wound makes her pause.

I rise without using the muscles in my legs. Look down — I'm hovering in the air! Close my mind to the impossibility of the situation. Extend both hands. An axe flies into my left, a short sword into my right. I look for the demons. They're huddled side by side, glaring at me.

"Come and get it, creeps!" I grunt, twirling the axe like a baton.

"A clever maneuver," Lord Loss notes, clapping drily. "Did you teach him that one, Dervish?"

"Never mind the commentary," Dervish growls. "It's your move."

My eyes dart to the boards. Incredibly, dozens of moves have been made in the few seconds since the game began. Play is at an advanced stage on all five sets.

Artery attacks while I'm distracted. Faster than my eye can follow, he crosses the room, jumps, and drags down hard on my legs. I kick at him, but he scrabbles up above my knees. The teeth in his hands sink into both my thighs. I scream. Artery laughs. Vein yaps excitedly. Bill-E butts the bars of his cage with his head and tries to bite through them.

I collapse to the floor. Artery's shaken loose by the jolt. I kick him backwards. He barrels into a pile of charred books, scattering them, squealing viciously.

Vein's on me before I can get up. Her teeth clamp around my outstretched left leg. She bites through my shinbone. Rips her head left and right. Flesh and bone tear. My foot and ankle fly across the room. Blood pumps from the lower part of my left leg — agony!

Vein and Artery scramble to the wound. Immerse their faces in the spray of blood. Gulp it down. Push each other out of the way, hungry for the taste of me.

Shaking — going into shock — eyes rolling — room spinning — numb to the pain — watching the demons feed — defeated — dying.

"Use your magic!" Dervish screams. My eyes half-focus. He's standing, face ashen. "Magic!" he bellows again, as Lord Loss grins and takes one of Dervish's queens with a bishop.

Staring at the demons — their faces red with my blood — imagining their next attack — the torment — spurred into action.

I'm still holding the axe. Summoning all my strength, I lash out with it and bury it dead in the middle of Vein's hard, elongated head. The demon falls away, choking. Her strength deserts her. She falls in a heap. I've killed her!

I almost shout aloud with glee, until I spot Artery climbing on top of Vein. He pulls the axe out and pushes the edges of the wound together. Blood glows. The wound knots itself closed. Vein gets to her feet, shaken, but very much alive.

My heart sinks — then leaps. Dervish's cry makes sense now. If the demons can use magic to repair their wounds, so can I! While Vein's still recovering, I point at my severed foot on the other side of the room and will it back into place. For a second nothing happens. Then it vanishes and reappears at the end of my leg. Flesh, bone, and sinews meld. The pain is worse than when it was bitten off. But it works! Within seconds I have my foot back, and though it's sore as hell, it will serve.

I don't test my weight on the foot. Instead, I calmly spread my arms and imagine myself airborne. With slow grace, I rise. Tucking both legs up behind me, I face the demons, then stab at them with my sword.

Artery bats my sword away. Vein jumps into the air and snaps for my legs, but I'm too high. I laugh at the demons, then slash at them again. They scatter, Vein to my left, Artery to my right.

Bloodlust. Sensing victory. I chase after Artery. Hack at him with the sword — miss by bare inches. Hack again — closer. He races from me, wailing, tiny limbs waving in an almost comical manner. Throws himself to the floor in desperation. I have him! Hurling myself forward, I take careful aim with my sword, bring it screaming down, and . . .

. . . hit the strands of web at the boundary of the cellar!

Sharp resistance, like hitting a steel bar. Bones crack. Sword drops. But worse — I *stick!* The strands of web are coated with a gluey substance. It clings to my arms, body, legs. I'm a fly stuck to flypaper. Struggling. Trapped. Helpless.

Artery and Vein gather below me. Their faces split into evil leers. The teeth in Artery's hands gnash dreadfully. Vein's eyes appear beadier than ever. She grips the web with her human hands. Crawls towards me. Artery not far behind.

Thrashing — tearing at the web — trying to bite through the strand nearest my face. I call upon my magical abilities — wish myself off of the web — it doesn't work! Blind panic — the demons closing in — here comes the kill!

A CHANGE OF PLAN

✝   ✝   ✝

VEIN creeps closer. Artery slithers next to his demonic sister. Both growling softly. My cries die away to a terrified whimper. Watching, sickly fascinated, accepting my doom.

"No!" Dervish roars, and he's suddenly floating above the demons. Grabs each by the scruff of the neck and hurls them across the width of the cellar, where they crash into webs on the opposite side. He reaches down, grabs my arms, and rips me free of the sticky strands. Presses his fingers into my back where the bones broke. A warm surge of power — the bones knit together.

"This is unpardonable, Dervish," Lord Loss mutters from his place at the chess boards. "To abandon our game while it's in progress . . ." He tuts disapprovingly. "You have broken the rules of our agreement. I am now free to summon as many of my familiars as I wish and set them loose upon you and the boys."

"Wait!" Dervish roars as Lord Loss rises. "I'll return to the game!"

"Too late," Lord Loss sighs. "Besides, what would be the point? Grubitsch is out of his depth. Let us put an end to this sham. You have disappointed me, Dervish, but there will be other Gradys and other matches." Lord Loss extends five of his eight arms, picks up Dervish's kings from each board, and starts to crush them.

"What if Grubbs plays you?" Dervish shouts.

Lord Loss pauses. "That was not our deal."

"We'll make a new deal," Dervish hisses. "The game continues where I left off. Grubbs assumes my position. I pit myself against your beasts."

"Why should I agree to that?" Lord Loss asks. "I have already won."

"No," Dervish disagrees. "*We* may have forfeited the game — but *you* haven't won. You can take our lives now, quickly, or you can prolong the agony and savor Grubbs's desperation and sorrow as he loses to you."

Lord Loss's eyes light up at the mention of desperation and sorrow, but he hesitates before replying. "What if he doesn't lose?" he finally murmurs. "I will have sacrificed the pleasures of a certain victory for the humiliation of defeat."

"It's a gamble," Dervish agrees, "but Grubbs is a poor player. Our chances are slim. Imagine the satisfaction you'll extract as Grubbs slowly and painfully comes to realize he can't win."

"You make it sound almost irresistible." Lord Loss smiles thinly. "But what does the boy think?"

Dervish looks questioningly at me. I shake my head uncertainly. "I just want it over with," I sob. "We're going to lose anyway — why drag it out?"

"As long as there's life, there's hope," Dervish replies quietly. "And it's not just yourself you'd be playing for — it's me and Billy too. Will you throw away our lives without a fight?"

I stare at my uncle's cold expression, then at the howling Bill-E in his cage. Wearily, I nod. "I'll try," I mumble. "If Lord Loss agrees to it, so will I."

Dervish's head whips round and he glares at Lord Loss. "Well?" he barks. "Can you match this child's courage, or will you flee with the easy victory?"

Lord Loss rolls the kings around in the stubby layers of flesh at the ends of his arms, considering the proposal. Then, with a smile, he replaces them on the boards. "Come," he says, gesturing to the seat which Dervish vacated.

Gliding to the floor. Dervish sets me down. Pain flares in my left foot. I ignore it. Hobble forward. Gaze at the five boards, the ranks of white and black pieces, then into the demon master's cunning eyes.

Breathing raggedly. Clearing my thoughts. Trying to remember every lesson Dad and Mom ever taught me.

I sit.

✠ Instant peacefulness. An unnatural silence. I stare around the cellar, startled. Everything seems to have stopped. Dervish stands motionless, facing the demons, while Bill-E's frozen at the bars of his cage. Then I realize they *are* moving — only incredibly slowly.

"What happened?" I gasp.

"I have separated our time frame from theirs," Lord Loss says. "It allows us to play without distractions."

I watch as Dervish's right hand slowly comes up, fingers

unfurling, red flames streaking from the tips. Slower than snails, Vein and Artery break to the sides, out of the path of the firebolts.

"Come," Lord Loss says, tapping the middle board. "The fight is no longer your concern. Focus on the match."

With an effort I tear my eyes away from Dervish and the demons and stare at the pieces lined up in front of me. Assessing the damage. I immediately note that the game on the far right board is beyond saving — that's where Lord Loss took Dervish's queen with a bishop. The game on the center board also looks like a lost cause, with white down both knights and a bishop.

"Depressing, isn't it?" Lord Loss sighs, looking more miserable than I feel. "Dervish was not at his best tonight. His fear for you affected his game. I warned him about that, but he would not listen."

Lord Loss picks up the queen he took from the far right board and toys with it. "It's your move, Grubitsch," he says, "but take your time. There is no rush. Study the pieces. Plan a campaign. Search for openings."

I reach towards a rook on the board to my immediate left. Pause. Withdraw my hand without touching the piece. "Can I move any piece, on any board?" I ask.

"Of course."

I run an eye over the five boards again, then pick up a pawn on the board to my far right and move it forward a space. The battle's already lost on that board, so I might as well start there and treat it as a warm-up. Hopefully work my worst moves out of my system.

"Ah," Lord Loss nods. "A cautious approach. Very wise, young Grubitsch." He moves a knight forward and checks my king. "It will make no difference to the end result, but at least you may lose with some dignity. Perhaps that will provide you with a glimmer of comfort when you and your unfortunate companions roast tonight in the fires of my own personal hell."

✠ It takes Lord Loss nine moves to checkmate me on the far right. When he wins, my king melts into a foul-smelling white puddle. Lord Loss picks up the board, snaps it into pieces, and tosses it aside.

"Then there were four."

✠ Sweating. Fidgeting. Trying to concentrate on the boards. Eyes constantly flicking to Dervish and the demons, locked in slow-motion combat.

I'm trying to keep play confined to the board on my left — taking the contest one game at a time — but Lord Loss won't oblige. He makes a few moves on that board, then switches to another, then another.

Though I have a free run of the boards, I can't make more than one move on any board until Lord Loss has replied to it. So, if I make a move on the middle board, and Lord Loss then moves a piece on the board to my far left, I can't make a second move on the board in the middle — I have to wait for Lord Loss to move one of his pieces on it. He's tied by the same rules as me, of course, but it feels like the odds are stacked in his favor, as if I'm the only one restricted.

I've played chess like this before, but not often, and not

recently. Dad tried me on multiple boards when I was younger, saw I wasn't able to maintain my focus, so worked on improving my individual game. Perhaps he'd have tested me again when I was older — if he'd lived.

It's impossible not to think about my parents and Gret. Did Dad sweat this much when he faced the demon lord? Was Gret half-frozen in time, like Bill-E is now, unaware of what was occurring, but somehow sensing doom? Did Mom lose limbs to the familiars during the fight?

I move a wizard-shaped rook across the middle board. The game here seems lost, but I'm taking it slowly, hoping a route to victory will present itself.

"Oh dear," Lord Loss says, and my stomach sinks. He takes one of my pawns with a bishop, exposing my queen. I'll have to move her now, but that's going to leave my king vulnerable. Any half-hopes I entertained of winning on this board vanish.

"So sad," Lord Lord whispers, red eyes glowing dully. "To lose nobly is horrible — but to carelessly throw the game away . . ."

"Stuff it," I half-sob, knowing he's right, hating myself for surrendering so cheaply.

"You can concede defeat now, if you wish," he says. "I have no heart, but if I had, there would be room in it for mercy. I will let you —"

"I said stuff it!" I roar, cutting him off. I brutally push my queen to safety, then turn my thoughts away from the board in the middle and focus on the three on which I still stand a slim chance of winning.

✠ ✠ ✠

✠ Lord Loss doesn't finish me off on the center board, but chooses instead to flirt with me on the others, toying with me, threatening my major pieces, letting me escape, then slowly moving back in for the kill.

I'm playing through tears, fingers shaking, breath rasping in my throat. It's not losing that I despise, but doing so in such a humiliating fashion. I ignored Lord Loss when he spoke of losing with dignity, but now I understand what he meant. To crumble at the moment of truth, to allow your opponent to psyche you out, to defeat yourself by playing dreadfully — that's a million times more sickening than coming, competing, and being beaten fairly.

"I could chase you forever, Grubitsch," Lord Loss murmurs, once again sliding a queen backwards on the board to my left, when he could have pressed on with her and ensnared my king. "Perhaps I will." He smiles with evil pleasure. "Time can barely touch us here. I could make this game last an eternity."

I respond by moving a pawn sideways on the far left board. A blind move, born of exhaustion and resignation.

"I'm afraid that's an illegal move," Lord Loss says, putting the pawn back on its original spot. "But I'll overlook it this time. Try again."

"Why don't you just finish it?" I scream, picking the pawn up and throwing it straight at the demon's face. The pawn sticks in the flesh of Lord Loss's left cheek. He leaves it there a moment, while blood pools around it, then pries it free and places it back on the board.

"You should be grateful that I procrastinate," he chuckles, pressing a finger to the fresh cut on his cheek, then licking it clean of blood with his long grey tongue. "This is your final ever game as one of the living. It's only fitting that it should last a lifetime."

✚ Hitting brick walls. Every time I advance, Lord Loss drives me back. Every time I go after one of his pieces, he smoothly evades capture. Every time I fall back and group my pieces around my kings — inviting him on, in the hope he'll get arrogant and make a mistake — he circles like a vulture, patient, cold, mocking.

My temper rises and drops from minute to minute. I scream at him, turn my back, and refuse to play, then give in and beg him to end the torment.

Through it all he observes me with a slight, cutting smile, which spreads during my darkest moments, as he feeds on my sorrow with relish.

Since my cause is hopeless, I spend more and more time watching Dervish battle the familiars. He seems to have the upper hand — the pair are wounded in many places — but Vein and Artery are still active, tracking him, probing for weak spots.

"A nasty nick," Lord Loss notes as Artery makes a pass and catches Dervish's left hip. Blood sprays into the air in slow motion, each drop vividly visible from where I sit. Dervish's lips press tightly together into a pained wince.

"I think your uncle might succumb before you do," Lord Loss says, reluctantly taking one of my pawns. "As brave and resourceful as he is, he cannot continue forever."

"You'd like that, wouldn't you?" I snarl. "To see him fail. To be able to pin the blame on him and make him feel guilty. I bet

you'd tell him I was enjoying great success on the boards —
torment him before you let your slaves finish him off."

Lord Loss beams ghoulishly. "You see through me, young
Grubitsch," he purrs.

"I'm starting to," I mutter, and return to the game. I'm
reaching forward to move a knight when I pause, thinking
about what I've just said. I *am* starting to understand how
Lord Loss operates. He isn't a difficult creature to make
sense of — as Dervish told me already, the demon master
feeds on pain. He thrives on the misery of others.

"Continue," Lord Loss encourages me, nodding at the
knight. "That's one of your finer moves. You'll threaten both
my rook and queen. I'll have to do some quick thinking to
wriggle out of this one!" He laughs, as though my cunning
delights him.

But it's not my cunning he craves.

It's my suffering.

I withdraw my hand and jam it under the table, thinking
furiously. My wits and chess skills are no match for Lord
Loss's. I've tried all I can to upset his game plan and disturb
his style of play. But what if the answer doesn't lie in the
game? What if I can compete with him on an emotional
level and undermine him that way?

Thinking —

He's a parasite.

He feeds off the misery of others.

He takes delight in my failings.

Observing —

His smile, how it grows as my mood dips.

The glow in his eyes when I run out of ideas and break down in tears.

The eagerness with which he attacks, then withdraws.

Wondering —

What would happen if I robbed him of his grisly satisfaction?

How would he respond if I cut off his supply of desperate grief?

I close my eyes. Forget the boards, the game, Lord Loss. Think about Dervish and the speed with which he pushed me into this encounter. He could have prepared me for this in advance, told me about Bill-E and Lord Loss, worked with me on my weapons and chess skills, just in case he ever had to use me. But he didn't. He dropped me in it. No training or commands, except one simple, core piece of advice — don't act — *re*act.

Understanding clicks in. My eyes snap open. I've been going about this the wrong way! Thinking, plotting, planning — those are all the things Dervish told me *not* to do. He warned me to obey my instincts, let the magic flow, react to the lunges and parries of the demons. He was talking about hand-to-hand combat, but why shouldn't those guidelines apply at the chess board too?

I recall the way he launched into the game. No hesitation. No long study of the boards. I assumed it was because he had his game plan set clear in his mind before he sat down — but perhaps he didn't have one at all!

"Grubitsch?" Lord Loss asks, fake concern in his expression. "Are you well, my young friend? Can you continue?"

I stare at him wordlessly for a long, pregnant moment.

Then I laugh.

"Of course I can!" I boom, startling the demon master. "Forgive me for the long delay — I was trying to remember if I left the light on in my bedroom before coming down."

"What?" he blinks.

"Dad hated it when I left the lights on," I tell him, casually moving my queen on the middle board forward, presenting her to Lord Loss's rook. "Electricity bills don't pay themselves, you know. Your move."

Lord Loss stares at me, astonished, then down at the board. "That was an unwise choice," he mutters. "Born of haste, perhaps?"

"No," I smirk. "I knew what I was doing."

"You can retract the piece if you wish," he says.

"Really?"

"It is not normally allowed." He smiles. "But I will make an exception. Take your queen back. Recalculate. Choose a wiser course of action."

"Very kind of you." I pull the queen back six places to her original position, pause a moment — then move her forward into the exact same spot as before.

Lord Loss's face darkens. I throw my head back and rock with laughter.

"You would be well advised not to try my patience," he hisses.

"To hell with your patience," I jeer. "This game bores me. *You* bore me. Take my queen or drag things out — I don't care anymore."

"You wish to concede defeat?" Lord Loss asks with undue eagerness.

"Nope," I chuckle. "You'll have to come take me. And if you don't — if you play it coy, like you have been — I'll chase you. I'll give you no option but to rid me of my queens, rooks, and bishops. And you know what I'll do then, *old friend*? I'll giggle! I'll guffaw! I'll positively explode with every last scrap of mirth I can muster!"

"You've lost your mind," he croaks.

"No." I smile spitefully. "*You've* lost your juicy meal ticket. I won't play the sad, bewildered victim any longer. You'll never feed from me again. You can kill me, but you won't squeeze one further drop of pleasure from me, not if you keep me alive for twenty lifetimes!"

The demon lord's jaw trembles. His eyes flare with pale red light. The snakes in his chest slide under and over each other in a sudden frenzy. Then he reaches out, pushes his rook forward with a stubby, ill-shaped excuse for a finger, and knocks my elfin queen from the table.

In response, I look him straight in the eye — and laugh.

SPIRAL TO THE HEART
OF NOWHERE

✠ ✠ ✠

LORD Loss surrounds my king on the middle board —
checkmate. I giggle as my king melts. While it's still bub-
bling, I move a knight forward on the board to my right,
then sit back and twiddle my thumbs, whistling tunelessly.

"This show of indifference does not become you," Lord
Loss says stiffly, attacking my knight with a pawn.

"No show." I smile, switching play to the board on my far
left, shoving a rook deep into enemy territory, barely thinking about it, not pausing afterwards to check my opponent's
response.

"This is ridiculous, Grubitsch," Lord Loss says. He fakes
an encouraging smile. "If you throw the game away, you
throw your life away too. You are already two games down.
You cannot afford to lose again. You must concentrate. If
not, you and your uncle —"

"Chess is dumb," I interrupt. "Like all games, it's silly and
pointless. People who take it seriously are fools. I'm sorry,

but I can't pretend to respect your foolishness any longer, regardless of what's at stake."

The demon master's lips peel back from his sharp grey teeth. "I could reach across and crush you into a million pieces!" he hisses.

"But that won't silence my laughter," I giggle. "Have you moved?" I lean forward to advance a pawn on the board to my left.

"Leave that alone!" he shouts. "I haven't had my turn yet!"

"Well, hurry up," I tut. "I've wasted enough time on this garbage. Let's get it over and done with."

Lord Loss trembles. Starts to say something. Catches himself. Mutters darkly and takes one of my pawns on the far left board. Before he's placed it on the desk, I push forward the pawn on the board to my near left, and once again fall back to studying my thumbs, twirling them mindlessly, thinking about summer, TV, music — anything except Lord Loss, his familiars, and chess.

✠ Lord Loss isn't smiling any longer. His features are contorted with hatred. He takes long, agonized pauses before each move — not to drag the torment out, but because he's unsure of himself.

I think about cracking jokes or singing songs, but I don't want to go overboard. Indifference is infuriating enough. He's unaccustomed to opponents showing no interest in the match or their fate. He's had long, delicious decades of pressure contests, feeding off the anxiety of those he faces, growing strong on it. He doesn't know how to cope with a vacant, yawning teenager.

I don't play blindly, but I play recklessly, pushing forward on all three boards, taking wild chances, surrendering myself to the random mechanics of chess. I'm presenting Lord Loss with more chances to finish me off than he could have ever dreamed of — but he fails to capitalize on them. He's too agitated to press for the kill. He fumblingly takes a few of my pieces but doesn't follow up on the captures.

And then *I* start taking *his* pieces.

I capture pawns first, a few on each board. I line them up in neat little rows, toying with them while he contemplates his moves. Then one of his knights falls prey to my queen on the board to my right. On the far left board I take a rook and bishop in quick succession. While he struggles to shore up his defenses on that board, I push my queen ahead on the board next to it — straight into the path of a black bishop.

Lord Loss gasps, his face lighting up. He sweeps the bishop forward, giggling intensely, eyes shining evilly.

I snort at the demon master's pleasure and slip a knight in behind his bishop. "Check."

He freezes. Stares at the knight, then his king, then the captured queen in the mangled palm of his hand. His jaw quivers, then firms. "A clever strategy," he commends me with icy politeness.

"Actually, I only saw the opening as you were removing my queen," I answer honestly. "Lucky, I guess — though luck always plays a part in childish games like these."

Lord Loss turns his face away in disgust. "You are a disgrace to the game," he growls.

"So punish me," I goad him. "Make me pay. Put me in my place." I adopt a very young child's challenging tone. "Dare ya!"

He hisses. Fixes his gaze on the boards. Studies them feverishly.

I pick at the nail of my left index finger and wonder if I should start using clippers instead of scissors.

✠ The balance of power lurches wildly between us. Lord Loss works hard to take three of my pawns. I respond by idly chasing his king with my knight on the board to my left, the one on which I lost my queen. He blocks my path, attacks my knight, and does all he can to repulse me, but I hang in there, amused by his failure to capture my knight. After a while I start thinking how lonely he looks, a single white knight stranded amidst a sea of black, and to provide him with company, I press forward with a bishop and a rook.

Lord Loss throws everything into smashing the three white irritants. He abandons attack completely and chases my knight, bishop, and rook as though they were responsible for some personal insult. After several frenzied twists and cutbacks, he traps my bishop and chuckles fiercely. "Next move — it's mine!"

"I reckon you're right," I sigh, then grin impishly and push a pawn forward. I'm not quite sure how it got there, but it's now only one space away from the end of the board, where I can exchange it for any piece I like. "But on the move after that, my pawn becomes a queen — much preferable to a bishop, don't you think?"

Lord Loss stares at the pawn, then the knight, then back at the pawn.

Two of his spare arms unfold around him. He covers his eyes. And moans.

✠ ✠ ✠

✠ "Checkmate."

I mutter the word emotionlessly and scratch my left elbow. "Can I make your king melt?" I ask curiously.

Lord Loss doesn't respond. His eyes are fixed on the trapped king on the board to my left, as though he can spot a way out if he looks at it long enough.

"I asked if I could make your —"

The black king explodes into tiny shards. I duck to avoid the flying bits of crystal. When I look again, Lord Loss's face is peppered with shiny splinters. Blood trickles from the cuts.

"You should take more pride in your appearance," I tell him. "You'll never attract girls with an ugly mug like that."

"I'll see you suffer for this," he says hoarsely, red eyes bulging. "Win or lose, I'll find a way to pay you back for the insults you've dealt me tonight."

"I don't know what you're talking about," I smile. "It surely can't be an insult to show no interest in a game in which I *have* no interest."

"Later," Lord Loss hisses, head shaking violently. "Later!"

He turns to the board on my right — the one with the Incan pieces — and broods over it in menacing silence, collecting his thoughts.

✠ He pushes me hard on the Incan board. Slow but steady advances. Cutting off my avenues of attack. Forcing me back. Pegging me to my own half.

I take no notice of the mounting threat. When I can't

move forward, I slide sideways, dancing out of the path of his soldiers, shrugging it off when he captures one of my rooks, laughing as my knights leap clear of the closing net.

Lord Loss's breath thickens the closer he gets to victory. Bloody sweat seeps from his pores. He twitches on his chair.

I ignore the danger I'm in. Keep one eye on Dervish as I shift a pawn forward. He's locked in close-quarters combat with the familiars, holding Artery away from his throat at arm's length, while Vein chews on his left leg. It looks serious, but I observe with cool disinterest.

Lord Loss grunts contentedly and takes my pawn. A path is opening up to my king. Another few moves and I'll have to sacrifice my queen.

"You're not laughing now," Lord Loss notes sadistically.

"Only because my laughter seems to disturb you," I smile sweetly, sending one of my knights to the right of the board, to cover my queen.

Lord Loss brings up a rook, blocking my queen's path of retreat. I move my knight again, lodging it between my queen and his rook. Grinning wickedly, he swiftly takes my knight with a pawn.

I wince — then wink. "I can't believe you fell for that one," I chortle.

Picking up my queen, I slide her diagonally far up the board, through the gap left by the pawn he moved when capturing my knight — and knock Lord Loss's black queen clean off the table.

His breath stops. His mouth closes. His stomach rumbles.

"Checkmate in four moves," I note drily. "Or is it three?"

In response, Lord Loss picks up his king and crushes it softly between his mangled fingers.

"Two-two," he croaks, and turns to the board on my far left — the final board — the decider.

✠ Lord Loss moves his pieces sluggishly. He plays with sad remoteness, face cast in dull misery, flinching every time I capture one of his pieces, handing the game to me without a real fight.

I feel a bubble of joy rising in my chest — and swiftly move to burst it. If I show any emotion now, he might seize upon it and revive with a flourish. Although it's difficult, I remain detached, moving my pieces instinctively, automatically, not dwelling upon thoughts of victory.

Gradually I rip his defenses to shreds. I check his king and he beats a sad retreat. For a couple of moves he threatens my queen, but then I drag her out of the way and check him again, with a rook. For a second time his king is forced to flee.

A short while later I trap him on the left side of the board. He's caught between my queen, two knights, and a bishop. He starts to move his king. Pauses. Does a double-take. Sighs deeply and slowly tips the king over.

"Checkmate," he intones morosely.

I blink — I hadn't seen it. "Are you sure?" I ask, frowning.

In response he pushes himself away from the table and floats out of his chair, face impassive.

Real time crashes over me. I'm hit by a wave of hot air. Sounds — Bill-E's howls, the snapping of Vein and Artery's teeth, Dervish's grunts. I spin. My uncle's on the floor, furiously wrestling with the demons. Blood everywhere. His left leg cut to ribbons. His right hand chewed off.

"Stop them!" I scream, darting to Dervish's aid.

Artery hears me, turns, and snarls. Spreads his hands wide — morsels of Dervish's flesh caught between his teeth. Rises to meet me.

"Peace, Artery," Lord Loss says, and the demon stops. "Cease, Vein," he commands, and the crocodile-headed monster quits chewing on Dervish's arm and looks questioningly at her master. "I have been beaten. We must respect the rules of the game."

The demons chatter and gibber madly. The flames in Artery's eyes flare and he hisses at his lord, shaking his head negatively. Vein snaps her jaws open and shut, then turns again on Dervish.

"You will obey me," Lord Loss says softly, "or I shall have your heads."

The demons pause. Then Vein clamps her teeth around Dervish's arm. Dervish screams. A blinding red light fills the cellar. I shut my eyes and cover my face with my arms. When I dare look again, Vein's lying in scraps of bloody flesh around my uncle. Artery has backed up to one of the webs and is whimpering fearfully.

Lord Loss floats over to Dervish and studies him blankly as he sits up and sets to work on his injuries, using magic to patch himself back together.

"I won," I remark, carefully approaching my preoccupied uncle, wary of Lord Loss — he might have killed the rebellious Vein, but I still don't trust him.

"So I see," Dervish says, not glancing up from his wounds.

I'm bitterly disappointed by his reaction. I expected cheers and tears, hugging and back-slapping — not this.

"You needn't sound so excited about it," I sniff.

Dervish looks up at me. A thin smile crosses his lips, then vanishes. "I'm delighted, Grubbs," he sighs. "Truly. But this isn't over for me. I have to fight Lord Loss now, and it's a fight I probably won't win. So while I'm ecstatic for you and Billy, I'm a little too worried about myself to celebrate."

"What are you talking about? We won. I beat him. We can . . ."

I stop, recalling the full rules of the challenge. Lord Loss is under oath to cure the person affected by lycanthropy if he loses at chess — but the one who beats him has to travel to the Demonata's universe and fight him there.

"But *I* beat him!" I cry, stooping to catch Dervish's eye. "*I'm* the one who has to go with him and —"

"No," Dervish interrupts. "The player always goes, while the one who fought the familiars remains. But since we swapped roles, we can choose who goes and stays. Isn't that right?" he asks Lord Loss.

Lord Loss nods slightly. "It is an ambiguous point, but I have had enough of the boy. I shall seek him out some other time. As I vowed, he will pay for his humiliation of me, but for now I wish only to wash my hands of him."

"But you're wounded!" I protest. "You're not fit to fight anymore. Let me. I know how to beat him. I can do it. I'll —"

"This isn't a debate," Dervish says gruffly. He grips both my hands in his and squeezes tightly. "You performed brilliantly on the boards, Grubbs, but this is a different matter.

He's far stronger in his own universe than he is here. Leave it to me, OK?"

Tears roll down my cheeks unchecked. "I don't want to lose you," I sob.

"But you must," he says, smiling. "At least for a while." He finishes healing himself and stands, groaning loudly. Turns to Lord Loss. "The cure?"

Lord Loss sneers. "I had not forgotten." He floats across the room to the cage. Bill-E backs away, snarling fitfully, but at a gesture from the demon master he flies across the cage and thrusts his arms through the bars. Lord Loss wraps two of his own arms around Bill-E's and slides the other six through the bars of the cage, encompassing the struggling werewolf. He exerts pressure, until Bill-E goes stiff, then presses his face forward, places his lips over Bill-E's, and exhales heavily, as though giving the kiss of life.

Bill-E's fingers fly out rigidly, then curl up into tight fists. His legs shake fitfully, then go slack. After ten or twelve seconds, Lord Loss breaks contact and releases Bill-E. He floats backwards, coughing and spitting. Bill-E teeters on his feet a moment, then crumples to the floor.

I start towards my brother, concerned. Dervish stops me. "Wait. He'll be OK. There are things I must tell you before we say goodbye." I face my uncle, who speaks quickly. "You know where the forms, credit cards, and contact numbers are. Use them. Act swiftly. Don't be ashamed to ask for help. And don't let the authorities take you away from here. They might interfere when they discover the condition I'm in, seek to separate you from me. Don't let them." His face is grim. "Lord Loss has threatened you — that's serious. He can't harm you in Carcery Vale — as long as you stay out of this cellar — but you're vulnerable elsewhere. In time you'll learn spells to protect yourself — friends of mine will help — but for now you mustn't leave the Vale."

"What can I do to stop them?" I ask.

"Stand up to them. Sic my lawyers — *your* lawyers — on them. Be brave. Prove you're fit to live independently. Don't give them any excuse to take you away. Meera will help — if she recovers — but you'll have to do a lot of it yourself."

Lord Loss has drifted to the edge of the cellar while we've been talking. He's floating in front of a thick bank of webs, gesturing at them with all eight arms, muttering something inhuman. Artery has crept up beside his master and squats sullenly next to him.

As I watch, the webs shimmer, then twist in a clockwise direction, winding and wrapping together. The center of the web pulses outwards a couple of times, then stretches backwards at lightning speed, cutting a path through the layers of webs behind it, creating an impossibly long, rotating funnel from the cellar to some indefinite point beyond.

"Take care of Billy," Dervish says. "He won't remember any of this. It's up to you how much you tell him. I won't advise you one way or the other on that point. If you start to change . . ." He hesitates, then presses on. "Meera and one of my other friends might challenge Lord Loss on your behalf. If you want to make a fight of it, ask Meera, and she can —"

"No," I interrupt softly. "I won't put anybody else through this. It wouldn't be fair. If the curse hits me, I'll abandon myself to it, call in the Lambs. But I won't ask anyone to face Lord Loss for me."

Dervish smiles wanly. "You might lose some of those noble ideals when you get a bit older." His smile softens. "But I hope not."

"It is time, Dervish Grady," Lord Loss says. The spiraling funnel he's created glows redly, the webs revolving rapidly. Artery leaps onto the web at the rim of the funnel. He's sucked into it instantly. Spins around several times, head over heels, then vanishes down the funnel's maw, never to be seen in these parts again — I hope.

"*Must* you go?" I sob, clutching Dervish's hands.

"Yes," he answers simply. "If I refused, he could bring his hordes of familiars through and destroy us all."

"How will I know . . . if you're . . . successful?" I gulp.

"As long as I'm fighting, I'll be an emotionless shell here," he says. "If I lose, that won't change, and you'll never know — I'll simply die of old age. But if I win . . ." He winks. "Don't worry — you'll soon find out!"

Dervish faces Lord Loss and the funnel. Takes a deep breath. Holds it. Lets it out nervously. "Remember, Grubbs," he mutters. "Don't give up on me. No matter how much time passes — even if it's decades — there's always hope."

"I'll look after you," I promise, weeping uncontrollably.

"Your Mom and Dad would have been proud of you tonight," Dervish says. "Gret too."

With that, he turns his back on me and marches to the funnel. Lord Loss bows politely as he approaches, then unfolds all eight of his arms and strikes for Dervish's throat. Dervish ducks swiftly, avoiding the demon master's lunge.

"Uh-uh!" he laughs. "You won't make that quick a finish of me!"

Leaping over the demon, he grabs hold of a thick strand of web, spins around, hollering wildly, then disappears down the funnel, becoming a speck, then nothing.

Lord Loss floats towards the opening. Glances back at me, eyes cold and hateful. "In the past, I've respected those who bested me," he snarls. "But you belittled both the game and me. I will be keeping a close watch on you, Grubitsch Grady, and if you ever —"

"My name's Grubbs," I grunt, cutting him short. I step forward, wiping tears from my face. "Now piss off back to your own world, you motherless scum, and save your threats for those who care."

For a moment it looks like he's going to abandon protocol and rip me to shreds. But then he snarls, whirls away from me, and hurls himself into the funnel of webs. There's a flash. The world turns red, then black. The webs fade. The funnel blinks out of existence. Walls and ceiling slowly return.

It ends.

THE CHANGE

✠　✠　✠

WORKING numbly. A quick trip to the house to fetch new candles. Then I sweep debris — broken chess boards and pieces — out of the way. Methodical. Chasing every last splinter and shard. Stacking them neatly against the walls. Need to keep active. Not dwelling on the game or the fight — or Dervish.

His body rematerialized as reality returned. But only his body — not his mind. He stands by the wall to my left, vacant, unresponsive, eyes glazed over.

Bill-E regains consciousness — and humanity — as I'm coming towards the end of my big cleanup. "Where am I?" he mutters. "What's happening?" He stands shakily and stares at the bars of the cage. His voice rises fearfully. "What am I doing here? Where's Dervish? What's —"

"It's OK," I shush him, fetching the key and unlocking the door. "Dervish is over by that wall. There's no need to be afraid."

Bill-E stumbles out of the cage and glances nervously at

the eerily motionless man in the candle-lit shadows. "What's the story?" he asks. "The last thing I remember is following Dervish — then nothing."

I haven't thought about what I'm going to tell Bill-E. So I say the first thing that comes into my head.

"We were right — Dervish was a werewolf. He knocked you out and brought you here. I tracked him and fought with him. He recovered. He was grief-stricken when he realized what he'd done — the change had never affected him this way before. He gave me a book with a spell in it and told me to cast it."

"What sort of a spell?" Bill-E asks, edging closer to Dervish.

"A calming spell," I improvise. "He'd been saving it for an emergency. It stops him from turning into a werewolf — but it also robs him of his personality. He's like a zombie now. He can't speak or respond. I don't know how long he'll stay that way — maybe forever. But if he recovers, he'll be safe. He won't change again."

Bill-E waves a hand in front of his uncle's eyes — Dervish doesn't blink. He's crying when he looks at me. "I didn't want this!" he sobs. "I wanted to stop him from harming people, but not this way!"

"There was no other solution, short of killing him," I answer quietly. "Dervish had controlled the beast all these years, but it had grown stronger and was close to overwhelming him."

"And you don't know how long he'll be like this?" Bill-E asks.

I shake my head. "A week. A year. A decade. There's no telling."

Bill-E smiles weakly. "He must have really loved me to do this to himself," he notes proudly. "Only a father would act this selflessly."

I start to tell Bill-E the truth — that Dervish is his uncle, my dad was his dad, I'm his brother — then stop. What would it achieve? If I told him, he'd have to come to terms with his real dad's death and being an orphan. This way, he believes he's not alone. I think it's better to have a zombie for a father than no father at all.

"Yeah," I nod tiredly. "He was your dad. No doubt about it." Stepping forward, I take hold of one of Dervish's hands and press the other into Bill-E's. "Now let's get the hell out of here — this place gives me the creeps."

✠ Days.

Meera recovers the following afternoon. No memory loss or serious injury. I tell her the whole story while Bill-E's at home with Ma and Pa Spleen. She weeps when she sees Dervish. Cradles his face. Calls his name. Scours his eyes for a trace of who he was.

Nothing.

✠ Weeks.

Lawyers. Social workers. Bankers.

Meera goes through Dervish's drawers with me. Sets the bureaucratic wheels in motion. My world becomes a flurry of legal papers and professional advice. Concerned officials kept at bay by Dervish's lawyers. Regular inspections. Visits from doctors and welfare workers. Tests. Under observation. Having to prove myself capable of looking after both myself and my uncle.

Dervish isn't that difficult to care for. I lay out his clothes each night and dress him as soon as he wakes in the morning. He can go to the toilet himself, once I point him the right way. When I lead him down to breakfast, he sits and eats. After that he does whatever I tell him — rests, or exercises, or walks with me to the Vale to stock up on supplies and prove to everybody that he's healthy and unharmed. He's empty, distressingly so, and I have to spend a lot of time on him.

But I can cope.

�֍ Months.

Autumn trundles round and I have to start school. Leaving Dervish alone in the house. I'm nervous the first few days, worrying about him, but when I realize he can't come to harm, I relax and settle down.

I sit next to Bill-E in most classes. (I've had to repeat a year, to make up for all the work I missed.) We get on better than ever. Occasionally he'll make mention of that night in the forest and cellar, but I always change the conversation quickly — I have no wish to dwell on such matters.

I enjoy school, and making friends — even homework! This is reality, the normal, dull, everyday world. It's great to be back.

✖ A year.

I grow four inches. Broaden. I was always large for my age — now I'm positively massive. And still growing! Bill-E calls me the Impeccable Hulk, and refers to the two of us as Little and Large.

He spends a lot of weekends with Dervish and me, watching DVDs and MTV. He says we should hold a party and invite some girls over — says we could act like lords in a castle. Talks of getting a monocle for his lazy left eye and crowning himself King Bill-E the First. I just smile and say nothing when he starts up with fantasy stuff like that. Of course I'm interested in girls, but I'm not ready for dating yet. One step at a time. The demons were scary, but girls — well, girls are really terrifying!

Dervish hasn't changed. As lifeless as ever, eyes blank, never smiling or frowning, laughing or crying. I talk to him all the time, telling him about school, discussing TV shows, running math problems by him. He never shows any sign that he understands, but it's comforting to treat him like an ordinary person. And maybe, somewhere far away, in the midst of bloody battle, he hears — and perhaps it helps.

I take him to the barber's once a month, to have his hair and beard cut. Buy new clothes for him every so often. Experiment with various brands of deodorant. Keep him respectable and in shape, so if he ever does return, he won't have cause for complaint.

Meera drops by every few weeks or so. Keeps an eye on us. Drives me outside the Vale to hit the bigger stores. I tell her what Dervish said, about not leaving Carcery Vale, but she says it's OK as long as she's with me. But we're careful not to linger, always back a couple of hours before the sun sets — demons are more powerful in this world at night.

She usually sleeps over when she comes. Bill-E jokes about it and says we're having an affair. I wish!

I often dream of Lord Loss and his familiars. I worry about his threat and what he'll do to me if he ever gets the chance. I block the entrances to the secret cellar with thick planks and dozens of nails. Avoid Dervish's study as much as possible, for fear I'd find a book about Lord Loss, which might somehow allow him to latch onto me and break through Dervish's magic defences.

But even more than the demon master, I worry about *changing*. Every time a full moon comes I sleep nervously — if at all — tossing and turning, imagining the worst, checking under my nails first thing in the morning, examining my teeth and eyes in the mirror.

I've memorized the names and numbers of the Lambs — the Grady executioners. If I have to call them one day, I pray that I have the strength to do it.

✠ The morning after a full moon. Fourteen months since my battle with Lord Loss. A crisp, sun-crowned morning. Stretching. Yawning. Thinking about school. Also about a girl — Reni Gossel. I like Reni. Very cute. And she's been giving me the sort of looks that make me think she maybe thinks I'm cute too. Wondering if it's time to hold that party Bill-E's been pressing for.

My cheeks feel sticky. Curious, I rub a few fingers over them. They come away wet — and *red!*

My head flares. Heart pounds. Stomach clenches. Thoughts of school and Reni forgotten. I fall out of bed. Desperately check under my nails — dirty with earth and blood. Hairs stuck to my hands and around my mouth.

Moaning. Slapping off the hairs.

I reel out of the room and down the stairs, almost falling and breaking my neck. Head spinning. Lights exploding within my brain. Vomit rising in my throat. Telephone numbers flash across my eyes. "And the wolf shall lie down with the lamb."

Into the kitchen. Dervish is sitting at the table, slowly spooning corn flakes into his mouth. I turn in circles, wringing my hands, tearing at my hair. My eyes fix on the telephone hanging from the wall. I stop panicking. Calm falls on me like a sudden cold rainfall. I know what I must do. Best to do it now, as soon as possible, before I lose my nerve. Call the executioners. Give myself over to the Lambs. Arrange for others to take care of Dervish. Bid this world farewell.

I start towards the phone, resigned to my fate.

A solemn voice behind me — "Grubbs."

I turn slowly, reluctantly, for some reason expecting to see Lord Loss. But there's only Dervish. He's holding up a tin of red paint, a small pot of dirt, and a ratty woollen scarf that has been ripped into hairy fragments.

"The look on your face!" my uncle says.

And grins.

The horrifying adventures continue in

DEMON THIEF

Book 2 in THE DEMONATA series

Available now
from Little, Brown and Company

Turn the page for a sneak peek. . . .

INTO THE LIGHT

✛ ✛ ✛

PEOPLE think I'm crazy because I see lights. I've seen them all my life. Strange, multicolored patches of lights, swirling through the air. The patches are different sizes, some as small as a coin, others as big as a cereal box. All sorts of shapes — octagons, triangles, decagons. Some have thirty or forty sides. I don't know the name for a forty-sided shape. *Quadradecagon*?

No circles. All of the patches have at least two straight edges. There are a few with curves or semicircular bulges, but not many.

Every color imaginable. Some shine brightly, others glow dully. Occasionally a few of the lights pulse, but normally they don't. Just hang there, glowing.

For a long time I didn't know the lights were strange. I thought everybody saw them. I described them to Mom and Dad when I learned to speak, but they thought I was playing a game, seeking attention. It was only when I started school and spoke about the lights in class that it became an issue. My teacher, Miss Tyacke, saw that I wasn't making up stories, that I really believed in the lights.

Miss Tyacke called Mom in. Suggested I visit somebody better qualified to understand what the lights signified. But Mom's never had much time for psychiatrists. She thinks the brain can take good care of itself if left alone. She asked me to stop mentioning the lights at school, but otherwise she wasn't concerned.

I stopped talking about the lights when Mom told me to, but the damage had already been done. Word spread among the children — Kernel Fleck is *weird*. He's not one of us. Stay away from him.

I never made many friends after that.

✠ My name's Cornelius, but I couldn't say that when I was younger. The closest I could get was Kernel. Mom and Dad thought that was cute and started using it instead of my real name. It stuck, and now that's what everybody calls me.

I think some parents shouldn't be allowed to name their kids. There should be a committee to disallow names that will cause problems later. I mean, even without the lights, what chance did I have of fitting in with any normal crowd with a name like Kernel Fleck!

We live in a city. Mom's a university lecturer. Dad's an artist who also does some freelance teaching. (He actually spends more time teaching than drawing, but whenever anyone asks, he says he's an artist.) We live on the third floor of an old warehouse that has been converted into apartments. Huge rooms with very high ceilings. I sometimes feel like a Munchkin, or Jack in the giant's castle.

Dad's very good with his hands. He makes brilliant model airplanes and hangs them from the wooden beams in the ceiling of my bedroom. When they start to clutter the place up, or if we just get the urge one lazy Sunday afternoon, the two of us make bombs out of apples, conkers — whatever we can find that's hard and round — and launch them at the planes. We fire away until we run out of ammo or all the planes are destroyed. Then Dad sets to work on new models and the process gets repeated. At the moment, the ceiling's about a third full.

I like the city. Our house is great; we're close to lots of shops, a cool adventure playground, museums, cinemas galore. School's OK too. I don't make friends, but I like my teachers and the building — we have a first-rate lab, a projection room, a massive library. And I never get bullied — I roar automatically when I'm fighting, which isn't good news for bullies who don't want to attract attention!

But, sweet as life should be, I'm not happy. I feel lonely. I've always been a loner, but it didn't bother me when I was younger. I liked being my myself. I read lots of books and comics, watched dozens of TV shows, invented imaginary friends to play with. I was content.

That changed recently. I don't know why, but I don't like being alone now. I feel sad when I see groups of friends having a good time. I want to be part of them. I want friends who'll tell me jokes and laugh at mine, who I can discuss television shows and music with, who'll pick me to be in their teams. I try getting people to accept me, but the harder I try, the more they avoid me. I sometimes hover at the edge of a group, ignored, and pretend I'm part of it. But if I speak, it backfires. They glare at me suspiciously, move away, or tell me to get lost. "Go watch some lights, freak!"

The loneliness began maybe three or four months ago, but got really bad this last month. I'm not enjoying life anymore. The hours drag, especially at home or when I have free time at school. I can't distract myself. My mind wanders. I keep thinking about friends and how I don't have any, that I'm alone and might always be this way. I've talked with Mom and Dad about it, as much as I can, but it's hard to make them see how miserable I am. They said things would change when I was older, but I don't believe them. I'll still be weird, no matter how old I am. Why should people like me more then than now?

I try so hard to fit in. I watch the popular shows and listen to the bands I hear others talking about. I read all the hot comics and books. Wear cool clothes when I'm not at school. Use all the latest slang and curses.

It doesn't matter. Nothing works. Nobody likes me. I'm wasting my time. This past week, I've gotten to thinking that I'm wasting my entire life. I've had dark, horrible thoughts, where I can see only one way out, one way of stopping the pain and loneliness. I know it's wrong to think that way — life can never be *that* bad — but it's hard not to. I cry when I'm alone — once or twice I've even cried in class. I'm eating too much food, putting on weight. I've stopped washing and my skin's gotten greasy. I don't care. I want to look like the freak I feel I am.

✠ Late at night. In bed. Playing with the patches of light, trying not to think about the loneliness. I've always been able to play with the lights. I remember being three or four years old, the lights all around me, reaching out and moving them, trying to fit them together like jigsaw pieces. Normally the lights remain at a distance of several feet or more, but I can call them closer when I want.

The patches aren't solid. They're like floating scraps of plastic. If I look at a patch from the side, it's almost invisible. I can put my fingers through them, like ordinary pools of light. But, despite all that, I can move them around.

When I want to move a patch, I focus on it and it glides towards me, stopping when I tell it. Reaching out, I push at one of the edges with my fingers. There's no contact, but as my fingers get closer, the light moves in whatever direction I'm pushing. When I stop, the light stops. I figured out very early on that I could put patches together to make mosaic-like shapes. I've been doing it ever since, at night, or during lunch at school when I have nobody to play with. Playing with them more than ever recently. Sometimes the lights are the only way I have to escape the miserable loneliness for a while.

I like making weird shapes, like Pablo Picasso paintings. I saw a program on him at school a couple of years ago, and felt an immediate connection. I think Picasso saw lights too, only he didn't tell anyone. People wouldn't think he was a great artist if he'd said he saw lights — they'd say he was a nutcase, like me.

The shapes I make are nowhere near as fabulous as Pablo Picasso's paintings. I'm no artist. I just try to create interesting patterns that will amuse me. They're rough, but I like them. They never last either. The shapes hold as long as I'm studying them, but once I lose interest or fall asleep, they come undone and the pieces drift apart, returning to their original positions in the air around me.

The one I'm making tonight is particularly jumbled. I'm finding it hard to concentrate. Joining the pieces randomly, not making any real shape. It's a mess. I can't stop thinking about friends and not having any. Feeling wretched. Wishing I had at least one true friend, someone who'd care about me and play with me, so I wouldn't be completely alone in this big, scary world.

As I'm thinking about that, and getting ready to move on from the lights, a few of the patches pulse. Just a handful, in different places. No big deal. Lights have pulsed before, from time to time. Usually I ignore them. But tonight, sad and desperate to divert my train of thought, I summon a couple, study them with a frown, then put them together and call for the rest of the flashing patches. As I add those pieces to the first two, more lights pulse, some slowly, some quickly.

Sitting up, working with more speed. Interested in this new, flashing shape. I've never put pulsing patches together. Adding to the cluster, more lights pulsing as the piece takes shape. I put them in place almost without thought, on auto-pilot. It's like the way I roar when I'm fighting — I have no control over it. I keep watching for a pattern to emerge, but there isn't one. Just a mass of different, pulsing colors. Still, it's worked its magic. I'm focused on the cluster of lights now, dark thoughts and fears temporarily forgotten.

The lights build and build. A massive structure, much larger than any I've created before. I'm sweating, and my arms are aching. I want to stop and rest, but I can't. I'm almost obsessed with the pulsing lights. This must be what addiction is like. We had a couple of police officers come in to speak to our class last term. They told us about the dangers of becoming an addict, all the things that . . .

Without warning, the patches that I've stuck together stop pulsing and glow the same light blue color. I fall back from this new, uniform patch, gasping, as if I'd gotten an electric shock. I've never seen this happen. It scares me. A huge, blue, jagged patch of light at the foot of my bed. Large enough for a person to fit through.

My first thought is to flee, call for Mom and Dad, get out as quick as I can. But part of me holds firm. An inner voice whispers in my ear, telling me to stay. *This is your window to a life of wonders,* it says. *But be careful,* it adds, as I move closer to the light. *Windows open both ways.*

As it says that, a shape presses through, out of the panel of light. I'm too horrified to scream. It's a monster from my very worst nightmare. Pale red skin. A pair of dark red eyes. No nose. A small mouth. Sharp, grey teeth. As it leans farther forward, into my bedroom, its chest becomes visible, and the horror intensifies. It doesn't have a heart! There's a hole in the left side of its chest, and inside the hole — dozens of tiny, hissing snakes.

The monster frowns and stretches out a hand towards me. I can see more than two arms — at least four or five. I want to pull away. Dive beneath my bed. Scream for help. But the voice that spoke to me a few seconds ago won't let me. It whispers quickly, words I can't follow. And I find myself standing firm, taking a step towards the panel of light and its emerging monster. I raise my right hand and watch the fingers curl into a fist. There's a strange tingling sensation in my fingers, like pins and needles.

The monster stops. Its eyes narrow. It looks around my bedroom uncertainly. Then, slowly, smoothly, it withdraws, pulling back into the panel of light, vanishing from the chest upwards, until only its red eyes remain, staring out at me from within the surrounding blueness, twin circles of an unspoken evil. Then they're gone too, and I'm alone again, just me and the light.

I should be wailing for help, running for my life, cowering on the floor. But all that happens is my fingers relax and my fist unclenches. I'm facing the panel of blue light, staring at it like a zombie fixed on the sight of a fresh human brain, distantly processing information. Normally I can see objects through the patches of light, but I can't see through this. If I look around it, there's my bedroom wall, a chest of drawers, toys and socks scattered around the floor. But when I look directly at the light, blue is all I see.

The voice says something crazy to me. I know it's madness as soon as it speaks. I want to argue, roar at it, tell it to get stuffed. But, as scared and confused as I am, I can't hold myself back. I find my legs tensing. I know, with sick certainty, what's going to happen next. I open my mouth to scream, to try to stop it, but before I can, a force makes me step forward — after the monster, into the light.

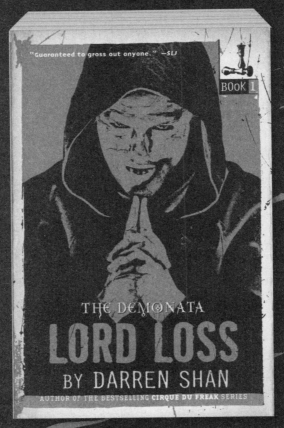

IN A UNIVERSE FULL OF EVIL, NIGHTMARES COME ALIVE.

THE DEMONATA

"Guaranteed to gross out anyone." —SLJ

BOOK 1

THE DEMONATA

LORD LOSS

BY DARREN SHAN

AUTHOR OF THE BESTSELLING **CIRQUE DU FREAK** SERIES

THE NEW YORK TIMES BESTSELLING SERIES BY DARREN SHAN

Little, Brown and Company
Hachette Book Group

www.darrenshan.com
Available wherever books are sold.